Two Seas

Work, family, old friends and rugby league

Geoff Lee

London League Publications Ltd

Two Seasons
Work, family, old friends and rugby league
© Geoff Lee

The moral right of Geoff Lee to be identified as the author has been asserted.

Cover design © Stephen McCarthy.

Photographs:
Front cover: Pennington Flash
Back cover: Batley versus Featherstone Rovers March 2009
Both photographs © Peter Lush

A CIP catalogue record for this book is available from the British Library.

First published in Great Britain in June 2013 by:
London League Publications Ltd, P.O. Box 65784, London NW2 9NS

ISBN: 978-1903659-68-7

Cover design by: Stephen McCarthy Graphic Design
                     46, Clarence Road, London N15 5BB

Layout: Peter Lush

Printed and bound in Great Britain by Charlesworth Press, Wakefield

About the author

Geoff Lee was born in the Lancashire glass town of St Helens in September 1939 on the first full day of the war, but it is believed that this was just a coincidence. He first worked at Prescot for BICC (British Insulated Callenders' Cables), but known locally as the Biggest Individual Collection of Comedians.

He called his first novel *Tales of a Northern Draughtsman.* It took him eight years to write, while he was still working as an electrical draughtsman for the CEGB. It then took him two years to find a publisher. It has a background of romance, Rock 'n' Roll and rugby league and its title was changed to *One Winter* as it is set during the terrible winter of 1962–63. It was published in 1998 and was followed by *One Spring,* set in the 1970s; *One Summer,* set in the 1980s with a background that now included redundancy; and fourthly *One Autumn* set in the 1990s with a background of work, family life and rugby league.

His latest novel, *Two Seasons* is set in 2002 and 2003. By this time Geoff had retired from work, mainly because there was no suitable work around and because he was recovering from quadruple heart bypass surgery.

Much of his content continues to be based on the old saying about work that "They could write a book about this place. It would be a best seller". He still enjoys listening to people talking on the bus and train, in the pub, at the match or wherever else he goes and so frequently bases many of his story lines on what he hears from people. He also draws much of his material from what he finds on the internet and in various local reference libraries that he always enjoys visiting.

He continues to have a great interest in rugby league and the way it is changing and expanding in both this country and worldwide. He still enjoys meeting old school pals, work mates and friends and hearing what had happened to them and telling them about what happed to him since they were last in company together, sometimes over 50 years ago!

He was intending to call this fifth novel *One January* because this would have given him the chance to write another 12 novels but decided against it. Since it he takes him between two to five years to do justice to his material, he would have been well over 100 years old when he was about to start on *One December!*

He also enjoys giving talks in libraries and once attracted an audience of nearly 40 people to Leigh Library, which so far, apart from having five novels published and selling thousands of copies, is the pinnacle of his career as an author.

Contents

1. "What's up with Elvis?"

"Good morning, my friend. You are looking rather miserable today. Whatever is the matter with your good self?"

"I'm having trouble with my landlord. I'm having trouble with my girlfriend and I'm having trouble with my bank because I haven't got any money in it."

"Well, let me give you a bit of advice, young man. If there is something wrong, and you can't do anything about it – don't worry, you can't do anything about it.

"On the other hand if there is something wrong and you can do something about it – don't worry, you can do something about it."

"Very good, Dave. I'm sure what you have just said will help our young friend enormously. Do you have any more pearls of wisdom to give to anyone else who has the misfortune to be with you today?"

"Yes Alan, I have something very appropriate for all those people who work in this joke of a drawing office. It's this. If you always do what you always did, then you'll always get what you always got."

"And what has that got to do with all us lot, may I ask?"

"What have all the drawings that you lot produce got to do with all the machines that I have to go and wire up all over the world?"

Dave Morris spent most of his time wiring up machinery that had been designed in Wilkinson's Drawing Office. He was well known for exaggerating what was wrong with just about every drawing he had ever been given. If it showed 200 electrical connections, but had just one connection shown incorrectly, he would complain bitterly that the whole drawing was totally wrong. But they all knew that he would always sort things out on site and so make life easier both for himself and all those idiots back home in the funny farm.

He took a print out of his bag, spread it on the table, and said that he would soon be taking this with him to a cotton mill in Egypt. How could he be sure that it was correct? It had been drawn on the second of May 2002 by C. Eckersley and had been checked and approved on the fourth of May 2001, by A. Greenall which meant that it had been checked almost a year before it had been drawn.

"The answer is quite simple, Dave. If you look carefully, that second date is actually the fourth of May two zero zero smudge."

"Well, I'm not sure that would stand up in a court of law, but I

1

suppose I'll have to accept it. You lot always have an answer for everything you do."

"Dave, you always question whatever you get given or get told about."

"And who is it that gets to travel all over the world while nobody here ever travels much farther than Lindsay's pie shop? Anyway, with that all cleared up to nobody's satisfaction, can I now have a large cup of coffee and can I also be invited to come on your office outing to Blackpool later last year?"

"You can indeed, my friend. Just put your request in writing and give us at least a week's notice."

"So what's been happening in this hive of inactivity while I've been out in the real world?"

"Well, for a start, your friend Cliff has been very busy."

"Doing what? I haven't seen him move yet and I've already been here far too long."

"While you have been away I have put him in charge of the office cactus. He has to keep moving it round every two hours to make sure it gets as much sun as possible. I've got to look after all the tomatoes on the window ledge in my office. They won't grow on their own, you know. They need watering three times a day and I've got a Busy Lizzie to care for as well. Then there's Colin. He spends most of his day fishing drawings out of the drawing cabinet. The rail is broken and they keep falling to the bottom."

"Well, it's clearly tough at the bottom and what's up with Elvis?"

"He's got trouble with his girlfriend, he's got trouble with his landlord and he's got no money to buy any sweets with. He's just told you that. I heard him."

"And where's my mate Tariq? Where has he skived off to?"

"He's in South Wales at Aberthaw Power Station. He'll be back next week or even sooner if he knows that you have gone away again."

"So, what other bits of news can you bore me with?"

"We've got a new member on our section now, someone who actually knows something about tariff metering and meter compensation calculations."

"Who is he? He must be a very clever man."

"It's a woman."

"Hell, I pity a poor woman spending all day in here with you lot.

2

Where did you find her?"

"That recruitment agency in Bury found her for us."

"Is she from Bury?"

"No. She's from Sunderland. She got a degree in Electrical Engineering at Salford Tech and now she lives at Bryn in Wigan."

"What's her name?"

"Jennifer."

"How long has she been here?"

"This is her second week."

"Where is she? I would like to speak to her and offer her my sincere condolences."

"You can't. She's not here today. She's in court."

"A criminal as well. She will feel at home in this place then."

"She is being called as a witness to a car accident in Ashton."

"Well I'm sure she'll witness a few things in here before she's been with you much longer."

They walked into Alan's office and the first thing Dave did was to walk round and stroke all his tomatoes.

"You know what Greeno, your office is becoming more and more like a greenhouse."

"Actually Dave, it's a Greenall house."

"I knew that you would say that."

"So did I."

"Where's Howard? Has he gone into hiding as well?"

"He's gone to prison."

"You're joking. What's he done?"

"Nothing."

"That's what most of them say."

"He's driven a neighbour to Risley to pick up his son from the Remand Centre. He's being let out this morning."

As they sat down Alan asked Dave where he had been for the last couple of months.

"I've been in Saudi Arabia, Tunisia and Ramsbottom, near Bury."

He flicked through the last few pages of Alan's desk diary and commented that they didn't appear to have much work on.

"We don't have much work on over the Christmas holiday, that's for sure. At the moment we're just ticking over, but once we get the okay for that bottle handling plant in Spain, we'll be very busy for

3

quite a while."

"If it is anywhere near a place called Calasparra and they want it wiring up correctly, they'd better send me out there. An old girlfriend from Earlestown lives there. I'm sure she would be very pleased to make me a nice Spanish breakfast now and again and again."

"And what have you been doing in Ramsbottom, may I ask? Not that it is any of my business, of course."

"That's right, Alan. It's not any of your business."

Alan Greenall had started work at the Wilkinson Engineering Works in Ashurst in 1955. At that time over 8,000 people worked there. Since then it had seen cutbacks, redundancies, division of the firm into two, complete closure of one half, followed by yet more job losses so that now the place was but a shadow of its former self.

What had happened over the last 20 years had also happened at nearly every other firm in Ashurst and also the nearby towns of Leigh, St Helens, Warrington, Widnes and Wigan. Fortunately, Wilkinson's had been taken over by a Dutch company called Koen Koevermanns in 1993. It was because of this that it had managed to carry on; but for how much longer, nobody could now be sure.

Alan had been lucky, never having been put out of work. Many of his former workmates from all over Merseyside and South Lancashire had been made redundant, some more than once. Then they had been told by well-heeled politicians to go and look for work that didn't exist, or might be totally unsuitable for them, or perhaps was suitable for them, but might be many miles away from where they lived.

By spending all his working life in one place, he had made friends with many great characters, people like Charlie Eccleston the office comedian from Thatto Heath in St Helens, and a big friend of the famous rugby player Alex Murphy; Mick Henderson the Wiganer from Platt Bridge; Sam Holroyd, always called Yorky because he had grown up at Mytholmroyd near Halifax; Tony – still managing a pub in Halifax; Les Earnshaw, now a famous author and living in London; Len Turner, the trade union man; Stan the war hero and Joan – the tea lady from Leigh and spreader of much gossip and scandal.

Most importantly though, it had been there, in 1963, that he had got to know the Welsh orphan girl, Thelma Johnson, who then worked in the Planning Office. Now they were married and had two grown up children, Rebecca and Robert.

The following morning Dave returned with his suggestion for a better way to do the work at Al Majeera. It would involve a few small changes that would only take a draughtsman of Alan's ability and good looks no more than a whole day to get done! He was right. Doing things his way meant that the job would take less time. This would allow Dave to do other things while he was in Egypt, like visiting the Pyramids and watch ships sail through the Suez Canal.

Halfway through the afternoon he returned to collect the drawings.

"Alan, have you stayed awake long enough to do those mods for me?"

"I've just got to print them off."

"No rush. I can wait. I am a very patient person, but there's one other thing as well."

There always was with Dave.

"Can I borrow a blank A4 pad?"

Alan opened the office stationery cupboard and as he gave the pad to Dave, he asked him if his dear little niece needed some colouring in pencils as well! Then he went into the Print Room and 10 minutes later returned and handed Dave a complete set of prints.

"Thank you very much, my friend. I'll remember this when I am making my uncle Ernie's will out. And if they've got a bit of spare electricity for it over there, I'll send you an e-mail when I find the first mistake. It'll probably be an hour after I've parked the camel."

Then he looked around the office and said loud enough for everybody to hear: "Do you know what? Cliff is stood in exactly the same spot as he was in all the time I was in here yesterday. Is he still alive?"

"I'm waiting for a phone call."

"Well remember this, Mr Platt: 'The things that come to those who wait will be the things left by those who got there first.' And on top of that I've just heard that things are going to get worse in here before they even get much worse. Toodoloo."

"Dave, before you go, can I tell you something that Oscar Wilde once said. Some people cause happiness wherever they go. Some people, whenever they go."

"I bet you didn't know that Oscar Wilde used to work in Wigan. One day he was told by some clever sod that no two snowflakes were alike. Do you know what his reply was, eh? Prove it."

As he walked away, Alan shouted out for everyone to hear: "Don't forget to bring us a nice selection of Pyramid Stones when you return from the land of the Fairies."

"What are they?" asked Colin, as soon as Dave had left.

"You know his partner Linda has a tourist type shop in Hebden Bridge. Well last year, while Dave was on a job in the south of Italy, he visited that ancient Roman town of Pompeii. When he got back home, he put the word around town that he had brought back with him some rare stones, ones that, when boiled in a mixture of sugared water and balsamic vinegar, were guaranteed to improve male performance. The next day these stones appeared in Linda's shop window and started selling like hot cakes."

"Or hot stones maybe."

"Hebden Bridge is full of hippies and all these daft buggers started buying them. What nobody knew was that he had dug all these so-called rare stones out of his back garden. Folk were paying a quid for them and it was a right little money spinner for Linda. No doubt she will be selling bits of the pyramids in a few weeks' time. I just love it when I get to work on a job with him. He's always got something funny to tell you about what he's done or where he's been."

"There used to be a comedian on the wireless in the fifties called Dave Morris. He was from up the North East, near Middlesbrough I think. Do you remember him?"

"I do, Cliff. The BBC used to broadcast a programme every Monday night from his club at Scotch Corner on the A1. Everyone else had a script to read from. He didn't because he was slowly going blind. What he used to do before they went on air was to get someone to read him stories from the local paper. Then he used to adlib his way through the show. That was all right for him, but all the others had to be quick witted about what to say next and keep as near as they could to the script."

"I can also remember a programme called *Educating Archie* on the Light Programme after *Family Favourites* on Sunday lunchtime. The main character in it was a guy called Peter Brough. He was a ventriloquist and he had a doll called Archie. On the wireless! Can you believe it, a ventriloquist on the wireless?"

"That's nothing, Cliff. I once listened to a programme on the wireless when I was a kid where the main turn was a juggler."

It was Dave again. He had returned, to see if he had left his pen in Alan's office.

"Dave, you made that up."

"Well, if that is all you can say about me I'm off as soon as I can find that pen that I paid a fortune for in sordid Arabia. I've got to fill out next week's timesheet with it."

As soon as Dave had left again, Alan walked back into his office and looked at his original plan for the installation of a HV circuit-breaker at Al Majeera. Then he looked at the way Dave had suggested doing it. His was a much better way, but that was hardly surprising. Dave had spent most of his life making things work, often by having to alter what a draughtsman had drawn badly or incorrectly. And with Dave having worked all over the world, Alan knew that what he would suggest was nearly always better.

It's nice when you are working with a guy like Dave and particularly when you are mates as well, not like a few folk that Alan had known or worked with over the years. One of the worst had been a Jig and Tool man called Cyril from New Brighton. Out of hearing, he was often described as having a head as big as Birkenhead and a mouth as wide as the entrance to the Mersey Tunnel.

Another one had been J. Arthur ('you can't do enough for a good firm') Wood, the assistant chief draughtsman. They say that you can tell how well respected and well liked a person was by the number of people who turned up at his or her funeral. Well in his case, excluding the men from the funeral company, it was none. Even the vicar of St Luke's Church had arrived late.

With Dave, it was just a pleasure to know him and work with him. However, he hadn't always been like he was now. He hadn't enjoyed his time at school or as an apprentice at the Gillarsfield Construction Company, a right cowboy outfit that was. Before his first year was out, he had had a right bust up with his foreman, but before anybody could get round to sacking him, the firm had gone out of business.

It was then that Dave had his great stroke of luck. Wilkinson's apprentice training officer, Jack Critchley, on hearing of his situation, had pulled a few strings and had him taken on in the Electrical Wiring Shop to complete his apprenticeship. Jack used to live in the same street as Dave and knew what a hard life his mother had had over the years, living with Dave's father, a man who had little time or interest in what any of his children ever did.

By the time Dave was 21, Jack had sorted him out. He then joined Wilkinson's Outside Contracts Division and started working on site and often abroad. Returning on the plane from a job at a steel works in Duisburg in West Germany, sometime later, he had got to know a nice young Yorkshire lass called Linda from Todmorden.

She was only just a Yorkshire lass though, because she had been born in a house that was less than a mile from the Lancashire border. That explained why they were now living together in Hebden Bridge, although not all the time because he was still regularly away on jobs that sometimes could last for two or three months at a time.

In many ways they had similar backgrounds. She gave the appearance of being a cultured, gentle, well mannered, well-spoken lady with great taste; but that was certainly not how she had been before they had met. On their third night out together, he had witnessed her other side. Waiting at a bus stop in Todmorden, they had been confronted by three drunken lads intent on robbing them. Before Dave could decide how to respond, he saw Linda floor two of the lads with well-aimed punches, kick box the third to the ground and stamp on the face of the first lad as he was struggling to get up.

Later that evening she told Dave about her younger days and how she had learned to look after herself. Her background certainly did not fit in one bit with how she now liked to spend her spare time, which was collecting foreign stamps and rare coins, reading and writing poetry, practising Tai Chi and singing madrigals while playing the cello.

2. A tale from Knowsley Road

The following lunch time Dave reappeared. He wanted a few small changes making to one of the drawings that he would soon be taking with him to Egypt. Then, as he began to eat his lunch, he said: "Alan, what's happened to Sacred Heart Church? It wasn't there when I drove down Newton Hill this morning."

"It was knocked down last month. Why do you ask? Don't tell me you've got a confession to make."

"Not today. I just haven't had any opportunity to be a naughty boy. Well not yet, although I have had a few exotic thoughts. Anyway while I'm waiting for something to turn up that I can't resist, I've got another question for you."

"Go on."

"What's happened to the *Rugby Leaguer?* My next door neighbour tells me that they don't print it anymore."

"It must have happened just after you went to Tunisia. Without any warning, the owners of the *Rugby Leaguer* sold it to *League Express.* The following day Ray French, Phil Hodgson and Dave Parker met a guy called Danny Lockwood who is the publisher of a weekly paper in Dewsbury. With some help as well from John Robinson from the *Sunday Mirror* and Martin Richards from the *Daily Mail,* in next to no time they had set up a completely new paper and called it *League Weekly.*"

"And how do you know all this?"

"Because I have friends in high places who keep me informed about what is going on the world."

"And I suppose you are going to tell me that this new paper comes out every week, does it?"

"How did you work that one out?"

"And I suppose that you are going to tell me that you still buy it every week."

"I do. I buy *League Weekly* and *League Express* every Monday. I like to know everything what's going on in the game."

"So when you've finished with it, can I borrow it?"

"You tight bugger. It only costs a quid."

"Fair enough, I'll start saving up for it."

"Do you know when the first copy of the *Rugby Leaguer* was

9

printed?"

"Oh, you're not going to start giving us another one of your history lessons, are you?"

"I thought you might be interested."

"Well I am, so go on, tell us."

"It was in 1949 and was first published in Claughton Street in St Helens. In the first issue there was a report of a sprint race between Warrington's Brian Bevan and the Saints winger Stan McCormick."

"How do you know that?"

"Because I've got a copy of it at home. My auntie Doris gave it to me when she was clearing out her house after my uncle Jack died. It'll probably be worth a few bob now."

"Well thank you very much for all that. I've been wanting to know that for ages."

"Do you know when *League Express* first appeared?"

"No. Probably the following week."

"September 1990. I've got the first copy of that as well."

"I thought you would have. I bet you've even got a copy of the *Magna Carta* in that spare bedroom of yours. But never mind all that. I want you to listen to me very carefully. I would like you to do me a little favour; well it's a big favour really."

He went on to say that when he arrived home the previous night, his sister Maureen who lived in London with her American husband John, were in the house. They had come up to stay for a few days and had brought John's father Elmer with them. In the 1950s, Elmer had been a GI at the American airbase at Burtonwood. While he had been stationed there, he had married a girl from Prescot called Janet. A few months later, he had taken her back to his home town in Ohio, where they had lived quite happily until a couple of years ago when they had moved to Italy and lived in Milan. Sadly, Janet had recently died and now Elmer had come to London to see his son John and sort out some family business.

Back in England for the first time in over 40 years, Elmer wanted to visit Burtonwood again. He also wanted to see the Beatles' old haunt at the Cavern in Liverpool, visit the Pier Head and watch his first live game of rugby league. When were the Saints playing at home next, would they need to buy tickets, could Alan drive them there? That was what Dave wanted to know.

The next home game was in three days' time against Wakefield Trinity. How did that suit Dave? Alan went on to say that he would be happy to take a half-day holiday and spend the afternoon driving him and Elmer round. After the match, they could come straight back to Ashurst and be able to leave from there early enough to pass through the M62 Border Control Gates while they were still allowing late night travellers to return to the 19th century!

So on Friday afternoon Dave, Elmer, Maureen and John arrived in Silkstone Street having spent the morning in Liverpool City Centre. Maureen and John then drove off to Southport to visit friends they had not seen for a long time. Elmer and Dave had something to eat and then the American's ride down Memory Lane began.

The first port of call was the area where the airbase had once stood; not much of it left now, the M62 went right through that bit of land. Then Alan drove towards Prescot, stopping on the way to show them Rainhill Station, the scene of the famous Railway Trials in 1829 and also Whiston Hospital, where Elmer had once spent time recovering from a motor bike accident nearby on Elton Head Road.

Then he drove along Warrington Road to see where Janet used to work in the Accessories Division of the BICC factory, though not a trace of the old place could now be seen. He turned right at the traffic lights in the middle of Prescot, and drove onto St Helens, going past Grange Park Golf Club, through Toll Bar and close to the house where Janet's sister used to live in Owen Street. By now it was well turned half past six and time to get to the ground, get something to eat and then enjoy watching the match.

They decided to sit in the main stand and it was soon unclear which version of rugby Elmer had seen on the TV. In fact, the American did not even know that there were two different versions of the game. Despite that, he thoroughly enjoyed what he saw on the pitch, once the main rules had been explained to him. He was amazed to see that rugby league players did not wear padded clothes and helmets and that each half lasted for 40 minutes with no breaks for any refreshments. He also enjoyed listening to all the shouting and banter from those sat around him. But he just couldn't understand the significance of the words 'Gerrum onside, referee' or the cruel references to the man as 'a blind bastard'.

After the game, which the Saints won comfortably 34–2, they went into the club shop where Elmer spent a small fortune. Then Alan drove them back to Ashurst, going through St Helens town centre, past Peasley Cross Hospital, along Robins Lane, under the bridge at St Helens Junction and on past the area where Bold Colliery and Bold Power Station had once stood. They returned to Silkstone Street, ate a few of Thelma's Welsh scones and then their visitors left. Elmer shook hands with Alan, kissed Thelma, and gave her an envelope telling her to open it after they had left. When she did, she discovered that the contents were three £10 notes.

Back in work the following Monday morning, things started off in a very sombre mood. The young trainee, Jason, usually called Elvis because he was the singer in a Manchester rock band, was in Salford Hope Hospital, suffering from some as yet undiagnosed illness. He had not been at Wilkinson's long and had kept very much to himself. Whether he was taking drugs nobody knew and where he lived was also a bit of a mystery. Some of the time it seemed to be in a house at Birchwood and sometimes in a flat at Eccles.

In the past someone from the Personnel Department would have visited the hospital to see how he was, but there were not enough staff to do things like that now. By the time Alan had rung up, Jason had signed himself out and left, never to be seen in Ashurst again. Looking through the drawers in his desk revealed little about him, other than his interest in Heavy Metal. There were a few tickets of music festivals that he had obviously been to and a notebook with a dozen or so names in it, most with a line scrawled across them and an amount of money written down. Did he owe them or did they owe him? Nobody would ever know.

A couple of days later, a detective from Manchester CID turned up and asked a lot of questions. Few, if any of them, could be answered. Jason was an unknown quantity. He didn't like football or rugby so that ruled him out of a lot of the office conversations. He didn't have much of a sense of humour, so many of the jokes and stories told went over his head. Neither did he show any concern or interest in the growing threat of war in Iraq, which was now becoming increasingly likely. In fact, he didn't seem to want to relate to the world in which he and the rest of his workmates were living. Not surprisingly he wasn't missed, he had been literally for the time he had worked there, a waste of space. He was able to use the computer well, but he didn't have much idea about the technical content of the paper drawings that he was putting onto CAD. Why ever had the Personnel Department employed him? But Personnel was now a law unto itself, not like when everybody's friend John Walker had been in charge.

Two weeks later Dave returned from his trip to Port Said. It had been very successful for all concerned. He had found no more than 20 errors on the drawings that he had taken with him and everything had gone extremely well on the social side too. He had been inside a pyramid, rode on a camel, swum in the Nile and been seduced by a belly dancer, twice, and that was just in the first week.

"So what has happened about that job in Spain while I have been slaving away under the North African moon, Greeno?"

"Nothing yet."

"So how have you lot been spending all your time?"

"While you were away, me, Cliff and Tariq spent a week finishing all the drawings for a water treatment plant up in Scotland. Then Mr Johnson comes in with a load of additions that he had been sent, but had never found the time to tell us about. So we had to change half of what we had done while he was in Amsterdam for yet another meeting, and as soon as he got back, he told us of more changes that he wanted doing and then get the job all priced up within two days.

"The following day we met the client who had driven down from Dundee. He told us that Mr Johnson had not understood everything that was needed, so we are going to have to start again and get it all posted up to him for a meeting that was due to start this morning. So not surprisingly we are rather pissed off with him, to put it politely.

"In fact Dave, the only good thing that I have enjoyed doing while you have been away is to write a little poem that I think will bring tears to your face and a smile to your eyes."

"Oh aye. Did you have a job number for it?"

"I did it during the lunch break, so I didn't need one."

"Well, let's hear it before Cliff starts reading bits of his paper out like he always does whenever I have the misfortune to be in here."

"It's this:
We the knowing
Led by the unknowing
Doing the impossible

13

For the ungrateful
Have been doing that for so long
That we are now expected
To do it all in half the time
With only half the info
And still get blamed
For it not being finished on time."

"Well done. I couldn't have put it that badly myself."

"So where are you off to next, Dave?"

"It's a secret. I'm not supposed to tell anybody. I think it's a government contract that the firm might have just won. All that I do know is that it is located at a secret nuclear bunker somewhere on the road between Leigh and Bolton."

He put his hand by the side of his mouth, leaned forward and whispered: "It's where the old Lancashire United bus depot was, but don't tell anybody. If they find out I've told you, I'll get sent to Hull."

"One good thing about Bolton, Dave, is that it's not that far to Ramsbottom for you to nip to."

"No, Alan. One good thing about Bolton is that what's there is even better than what was on offer at Ramsbottom."

He then went on to say how much Elmer had enjoyed watching the rugby and how much he had appreciated Alan giving up an afternoon to drive them round.

Alan's response was to say that he would be very happy to give up even more of his time if he got another 30 smackers for doing it.

"There's another thing too. He has become very interested in what you told him about how rugby league and rugby union had split back in whenever it was and wherever it was."

Alan's little history talk about what had happened at the George Hotel in 1895 had been told by him to many people new to the game and even to others who had watched it for years, but still didn't know much about it. Then Dave showed just how much Elmer was interested when he pulled five £10 notes out of his wallet and said: "He wants to read a lot more about it. Here's 50 quid. Can you get him some books to read about it? This is his address in Italy to send them to. But don't send them just yet. He won't be going back there before the end of September. He's gone over to Ireland for a few weeks. He thinks he's found out where one of his ancestors originally came from in the 1850s."

Alan had a good idea what he could buy for Elmer. Three very good books that he had read some time ago immediately sprang to mind. There was *Rugby's Great Split* by Tony Collins, *At The George* by Geoffrey Moorhouse and *Rugby's Class War* by David Hinchcliffe. Also there was one written by Mike Rylance called *The Forbidden Game*. That described how rugby league had been banned in war time France by the Nazi supporting Vichy Government.

Now where could he buy them all? Wardleworths in Westfield Street in St Helens might be worth trying first or maybe Trevor Smith's shop in Mesnes Street in Wigan. Both shops stocked a wide range of books about the game and Alan often visited them both. If they didn't have them in stock he was sure that Barbara or Trevor would be able to get hold of them for him. And if they couldn't, well he could always have a day out in Manchester and visit Sportspages to see if they had them.

"There's another thing too. You know that song the Saints' fans sing, the one that sounds like *Annie's Song* but with different words. He wants to know them as well. Can you write them down for him?"

"I'll do it now for you."

And with that, Alan wrote out

You light up my senses
Like a gallon of Greenalls
Like a kebab from Geno's
Like a good sniff of glue
Like a night out at Martine's
Like a split, fish and curry
Oh St Helens rugby
Come thrill me again.
Nah nah nah nah nah nah nah
OOH.

Then he said: "I'd sing it for you but there's a lady in the room."

Jennifer smiled at them both as Alan went on to ask Dave where he was going to next.

"On Saturday I'm going USA."

"Really? I didn't know we had any jobs on over there."

"Who said anything about work? Anyway I'm only going for a day."

"What? To America!"

"Who said anything about America? I'm taking our lass 'Uther Side of Accrington'. To Nelson actually. Have you not heard that one before? They often say that in Burnley. Her cousin is getting married there."

He laughed and went on: "I haven't met her husband to be yet although I have to say I feel a bit sorry for him after last week when I heard what happened to him a few years ago."

"Why's that?"

"When he was a lot younger, his parents abandoned him. Just threw him out and on his birthday too."

"How old was he when that happened?"

"32."

"He's a big lad, not like his younger brother. He's as thin as a lat. He's that thin, last week, he even fell through his string vest."

"Dave, have you been drinking?"

"Not yet, but I wouldn't mind a coffee now that you are offering to make me one."

Five minutes later Alan returned with two mugs and as he put one in front of him, Dave went on in a slightly more serious mode:

"Do you know that Tony Griffiths has come back?"

Tony was another commissioning engineer. He had been based in the Far East for over a year and had been working on power distribution projects in Indonesia, China and Vietnam. But now, he had decided to return to England and live at home in his house in Grappenhall on the other side of Warrington.

"He's earned a small fortune while he's been out there, though I don't think it's enough to pay off all the clothing bills of his wife and his three daughters."

"So where is he going to be spending his time now?"

"Probably stood outside the front of Dorothy Perkins shop for a bit, stopping any of them going in there again."

"Is he back in work now?"

"Not yet. He's having a week's holiday first. He'll be back next Monday, no doubt with a load of tales to tell."

What was it about all the people who worked for the Outside

Contracts Division? They could all spin a good yarn about every job they ever went on and with Tony having been away for so long, well it would no doubt take a long time for him to tell everybody about all his various escapades, dices with death, meetings with kings, queens, presidents and vice presidents of faraway countries and sleeping in strange beds, not always by himself.

But then no one would ever doubt that much of what he told them was almost certainly true. In fact he had proof of one of his most farfetched stories. It was a few years earlier when he had been working in the Philippines capital, Manila, on a project for the country's power generation industry One day he had been asked to take part in a high level meeting with the country's Minister of Power.

The meeting place was in the main government building. It just so happened that was also the location for a meeting between a number of representatives of various international bodies and governments. Around the time Tony was sitting in the reception area waiting to be called to his meeting, all the delegates walked past him and down a corridor into a large hall.

As they had all filed past, Tony recognised the American President Bill Clinton, the French President Jacques Chirac and two members of the British Government. Curious to the extreme, he had fallen in with some of the lesser important delegates and walked into the hall where they had all stood together and had their photographs taken. Later that day, one group photograph had been dispatched to press agencies all over the world. It showed Tony stood between the Prime Minister of India and the Foreign Minister of Belgium. You couldn't make it up, could you?

Yes, with Tony Griffiths back in town and working in the Wiring Shop, there would be plenty for everybody to look forward to.

3. A day out in Wigan

"Happy birthday, Mr Greenall, you old dinosaur."

It was Friday lunchtime and in two days' time Alan would be enjoying his 63rd birthday. To begin the celebrations he had invited all his section to join him for a drink in the Eagle and Child.

"So how long have you got to go now before you retire, Greeno?"

"Two years unless I have the good luck to be made redundant, which might be very nice for me, financially that is."

"It might be very nice for you, but it won't be very nice for any of us young ones."

"Are you looking forward to it, Alan?"

"Do you know what I'll say to you all when I walk out of this place on my very last day?"

"Will one of you remember to turn out the lights?"

"Thank God that's all over."

"It's been nice to have known you all."

"It's not been nice to have known you all."

"I could write a book about this place. It would be a horror story."

"Well, thank you for all those kind thoughts. Can I now assume from what you have all said, that I won't be getting a leaving present from any of you?"

"You'll get a free bus pass. What more do you expect?"

"Or deserve?"

"'Goodbye tension, hello pension', that's what I'll be saying on my last day."

"Don't bank on it, Alan. The way the Finance Department in Amsterdam run things, there might not be any money left for your pension."

"And if there is, it'll all be in Dutch money anyway."

"So boss, can you tell us what has inspired you to keep coming here every day for the last 50 odd years?"

"It can be summed up in three old sayings, Tariq. Never let the bastards grind you down. Keep smiling, it makes people wonder what you are up to and the early bird may get the worm, but it's the second mouse that eats the cheese."

"I'll say one thing about you, Greeno. I hope I look as good as you do now, when I am 72."

"Well actually Colin, at this moment in time I am still 62. Maybe you ought to visit that new opticians in Bridge Street."

"I think that you are all being very unkind to him."

This time it was Jennifer, the most recent addition to the Drawing Office. She had not been with them long, but had quickly added a whole new dimension to the place.

At this point they were joined by Tony Griffiths. On his second day back in work, following his long stint abroad in the Far East, a job had cropped in Slovenia that required his involvement, so he hadn't yet had any chance to talk to anybody from the Drawing Office.

"Greeno, since I am led to believe it's your birthday; I won't spoil it by telling you what an absolute cock up you lot have made on that job at Ljubljana Airport."

He sat down next to Jennifer and asked her if she worked in the asylum as well or was she Alan's new wife. Before she could reply he went on to ask Alan if they had built an airport in Ashurst while he had been away.

"No. Why?"

"On my way here this morning, I was driving through Sutton and saw a Gillarsfield Airport taxi coming out of St Helens Junction."

He then talked about his trip to Slovenia and how the place reminded him of when he used to play with his cousin Kevin on the Wigan Alps whenever he visited his auntie who lived at Bryn.

"Bryn, that's where you live isn't it, Jennifer?"

"Yes, but I've never heard of the Wigan Alps before."

"It was a slag heap, well three slag heaps, side-by-side. They were also known as the Three Sisters. You mustn't have lived there long but then you don't sound much like a Wiganer, do you."

"You're right, Tony. I'm not a Wiganer. I'm a Makem."

"What's that? A posh Geordie?"

"Not quite. I grew up in Sunderland, but when I was 17, my dad got a job at Heinz in Kitt Green and we all moved down here."

"And what do you do? Do you just make the tea?"

"Eh, Tony, she can do three things that you can't do. Computer Aided Design, meter compensation calculations and she's swum for the English University Women's team."

"Well I certainly couldn't do the third, but I bet I've done one thing that she hasn't done."

"What's that?"

"I've swum in Scotsman's Flash in me bare nack."

Jennifer looked a little puzzled.

"Do you not know what a flash is?"

"No."

"A flash is water in a hole that has been caused by mining subsidence, like a pond or in some cases as big as a lake."

"Well I've swum in the North Sea. Is that any good?"

"Nice one Jennifer. That's put him in his place."

"Did you do it in your bare nack?"

Alan explained that this was the Ashurst way of describing having no clothes on.

She replied by saying that she had been accompanied by her then boyfriend and a few members of a local nudist club celebrating her 17th birthday.

"I know who Jennifer reminds me of now. That tea girl from Earlestown we used to have. The one who went to Bradford College and then became a teacher. What was her name?"

"Hazel it was, Pete. Hazel Hutton. Who could ever forget her? I bet you didn't know that a few years after she finished here, loads of her kids started going to university."

"How many did she have?"

"About 60 every year."

"How many?"

"60. She's the deputy headmistress at St John's College."

By now they had been joined by two more of Alan's friends, both of whom worked in the Electrical Wiring Shop.

Mick was a six foot two 30-year-old whose weight rarely reached 10 stone. Eddie was the spitting image of Les Dawson, not in speech though, because he had grown up in Newcastle and sounded just like Jimmy Nail.

"Are ye ganning the match the night, hennie" asked Colin, in a terrible impersonation of a Geordie.

"I'll be ganning early just in case they are a man short and they need me. I always do."

The match referred to was not one involving Newcastle United playing at St James's Park on Tyneside. It was the Saints playing Leeds at Knowsley Road, just a few miles away.

As soon as they were all back in work, Jennifer asked Alan what he wanted her to work on next. She had received an e-mail from Cliff, telling her that the information he had given her the previous day about the boiler house alarms system at Aberthaw Power Station was wrong, which meant she might have to deal with that first.

Now, if Cliff worked in the company's head office in Amsterdam, or in an office some distance away, then that would be an acceptable way of communicating with her. But he sat next to her! How strange this seemed to an old fashioned draughtsman like Alan, but then not that surprising because they all now worked in a drawing office that did not have even one drawing board for anyone to draw anything on.

He told her to carry on with what she was already doing and so the rest of the afternoon passed without much else interesting happening. Finally, as they all walked out of the office at the end of the day, she shouted out: "Alan, don't forget to bring some birthday cake in on Monday."

Twenty minutes later he was telling his wife Thelma what had happened at work and in the pub that day. Then he asked her if she had organised anything special for his birthday on Sunday.

"All I am prepared to say at this moment in time is that the celebrations have been carefully planned and they will be starting first thing tomorrow morning."

"Where are we going?"

"To visit an ancient seat of Roman civilization."

"Oh, not Wigan again."

"How did you guess? We will be having our lunch in the Chippery in Market Street, famed throughout the world for its steak puddings, chips, gravy and mushy peas with a barm cake. We'll also be visiting Trevor Smith's bookshop where you can choose a nice book to buy, bring home, put on a shelf and never read until after you retire."

As soon as he had finished his evening meal, he began to get ready for the evening's entertainment. Thelma decided not to go with him to the match because a friend, who she hadn't seen for ages, was coming round to see her, so Alan went with Phil, his next door neighbour. They set off early and easily managed to find a place to park in Doulton Street. Walking up to the ground they could see there was going to be a large crowd.

As they reached Dunriding Lane, they had to wait while a dozen coaches carrying Leeds supporters drove past. As they approached the turnstiles, Alan saw a few familiar faces. Joining what was quite a long queue even though it was not yet half past seven, he was tapped on the shoulder by his old mate Eric Yates who he hadn't seen for ages. Alan had much to thank Eric for. It was his trickery outside the Co-op Hall that had led to Alan meeting Thelma on Christmas Eve in 1962. They had a quick chat about what each was doing now and agreed that they should go out for a drink sometime soon.

Once they were in the ground, Eric left them for his usual spot in the Edington Stand. Having found their place near the halfway line, Alan opened his programme and started to read out loud to Phil, the Saints team: Albert, Hoppe, Gleeson, Newlove, Kirkpatrick, Martyn, Long, Nickle, Cunningham, Shiels, Joynt, Stankevitch and Sculthorpe with Bennett, Edmundson, Ward and Higham the four subs.

"Well done, Greeno. Nice to see that you have finally moved on from reading *Peter and Jane* books."

It was Dave Tunstall, now stood next to him, accompanied by two other regulars. Dave had once worked in the Machine Shop at Wilkinson's and was a real Saints diehard. He had not missed a home game for years, something helped by living in Horace Street, which was within walking distance of the ground. He pulled a magazine out of his pocket and said: "Alan, have you ever seen this before? I've just bought it off a lad selling them outside."

It was *TGG, The Greatest Game* magazine.

"Not only have I read it, Dave. I've got all the back copies of it at home except the second one."

"I thought you would have."

"I also read *Our Game, Rugby League World, The Final Hooter* and *The Dropped Ball.*"

"I've not heard of the last two. Who writes them?"

"*The Final Hooter* is written by a bloke called Michael Wray from Birkenhead and *The Dropped Ball* is written by Tom Evans from the Ashurst Rugby League Supporters' Association. You'll probably know him. He used to work in the Paint Shop. I've also heard that Harry Edgar is planning on bring out a new magazine soon so if it's half as good as his *Open Rugby* used to be I'll be buying that as well."

Soon the curtain raiser involving two under-16 teams finished, and as the young stars of the future left the field, the voice on the tannoy blasted out the names of the players in both teams.

Soon the Leeds team ran out onto the pitch, greeted by a great roar from their supporters all bunched together at the Eccleston end. A minute later the appearance of the home team produced an even greater roar. There were now well over 10,000 spectators in the ground and they were soon to be well entertained by both teams. In the end the Saints ran out winners 38–18. John Kirkpatrick scored a hat trick of tries, Darren Albert, Martin Gleeson and Tommy Martyn each scored one and Paul Sculthorpe kicked seven goals. The way the Saints performed indicated that they would be in for a good season. The only bad thing as far as Alan was concerned though, was what Dave Tunstall had said at half-time. It was about a rumour going round the town that the club was considering leaving Knowsley Road, their home since 1890, and moving to a new ground on the site of the old UGB factory where his uncle Jack used to work.

"It'll never happen" thought Alan, but then that was more what he hoped and not just him, but many other supporters too. But these were all people for whom their memories and association with Knowsley Road were very strong. However, few of them knew how much of a drain on the club's finances the maintenance of the place was, but they all knew how bad the toilets were.

The following day was a good one too. They spent an hour in the Wigan Local History Museum in Library Street, a place full of information, photographs and records of life in early industrial Lancashire. Then they ate in the Chippery. As always, Alan chatted to the old man who ran the place. In appearance, Frank was like a character out of a Charles Dickens film, Alan would often say, ignoring the fact that Charles Dickens never made any films. Then they walked through Wigan Market to Trevor Smith's bookshop. Trevor was there and happy to tell Alan that he had three of the books he had rung up about; but not Mike Rylance's, which he thought he could get hold of. So Alan bought the three that he would be sending to Elmer, plus one for himself, a book of photographs showing railway sidings, slag heaps and long gone terraced streets in Wigan in the late 1920s.

Then they walked up to the Raven on Wallgate. In there was an old friend stood at the bar. It was Rita, who used to work in the Print Room. She had the same laugh she had always had all the time he had known her, but her croaking voice and permanent cough were proof of the effect that smoking 20 cigs a day since she was 16, had had on her throat and her health generally.

On Sunday morning, just as lunchtime was approaching there was a knock on the front door.

"Are you coming for a wet, Alan?"

It was Phil, wanting to take him out for a drink to celebrate his birthday.

"Just one pint Alan, dinner will be on the table at half one and there will be more refreshment for you to drink here," said Thelma.

Half an hour later he was back home. "See you later" he said to Phil, not having any idea when that might be. He walked into the house saw a great spread on the table that had been laid for four people. Was his son Robert coming round with his latest girlfriend or maybe his daughter Rebecca with Neil and their daughter Joanna? It was neither, both had sent their best wishes, both couldn't make it. Alan knew he would see Rebecca the following day because he was helping Neil install a central heating system in their house at Burtonwood.

He went upstairs, had a wash and came down 10 minutes later to see Phil, sat at the table along with his sister Sandra. She was staying next door while her house in Fenton Street was being rewired. Phil had said nothing all the time they had been in the pub, but then that was what a surprise was all about. It was also Thelma's idea of getting to know Sandra a little better too.

By the end of the evening, he was somewhat inebriated to say the least, having drunk four bottles of a German beer that Robert had left for him. No doubt he would wake up in the morning with a hangover and by the time Phil and Sandra had left, he knew that he shouldn't have drunk so much because of the physical work that awaited him in the morning.

By the time Thelma switched on the *BBC News*, he had had enough. There was only one thing that he wanted to do now. That was to fall asleep, something which, around this time of the day, he had been doing for the last 60 odd years. It was something that he was very good at too and well known for as well. But before he did move into the land of nod, he carefully put the books he had bought for Elmer in the bookcase in the front room and put the one he had bought for himself upstairs.

He saw the programme from the Leeds match on the floor where it had fallen and put it in a drawer. In there were a large number of programmes, some going back as far as 1947. That was when his uncle Jack had first taken him to Knowsley Road. He could still remember it; the visitors had been Belle Vue Rangers who wore blue and white hooped shirts. Uncle Jack had taken him a couple of more times after that and then he started going with three of his school pals. Although it had been good being with his uncle, it was much better in the Boys' Pen. He remembered fondly his uncle Jack. He had been a great influence on him then. He had acted almost like a father to him, his own father having been killed in the war.

In those days Alan's favourite players had been Jimmy Stott, Duggie Greenall, George Parsons, Alan Prescott, Joe Ball and the Australian Max Garbler. Except for Duggie, they would now all be living up in Heaven along with a different set of Saints to get to know and have some fun with.

He flicked through the programmes and saw one for a game he could well remember. It was the occasion of the Championship Final against Hunslet at Odsal Stadium in Bradford on 15 May 1959. Compared to Knowsley Road, Odsal was an enormous place. On one occasion in 1954 over 120,000 people had watched the Challenge Cup Final replay there between Warrington and Halifax.

For the game against Hunslet there had only been around 50,000 spectators present. The Saints had won handsomely with their star winger Tom van Vollenhoven scoring a hat-trick and the full-back Austin Rhodes kicking 10 goals. What a night it had been too. On the journey back, their coach had stayed for a few hours in Oldham. He had gone with a large group of mates and as usual they had all had too much to drink. He didn't remember much about what had happened after they went into the third pub, or was it the fourth one? One thing that he did remember though was sitting on Mumps Station with a lad from Eccleston waiting for the first train back to Ashurst on the following morning.

4. A day on the M62

It was a miserable day, not one for driving to Drax Power Station in North Yorkshire. On arriving at work, Alan collected a set of drawings from his desk, went into the Wiring Shop, to get the trolley he had loaded up the previous day and pushed it out into the yard. As he was putting all the gear from the trolley into the works van, along with the trolley, he heard the voice of Mick, the transport foreman.

"Tha can't park thur. Not unless tha's getten permission."

"I'm not parking here, Mick. I'm going to Drax in it."

"That's okay then, ewd lad, as long as tha going tomorrer."

"Well, actually I was planning to go now if that's all right with you."

"It's aw reet with me as long as tha can get thur and back by 10 o'clock."

"10 o'clock tonight?"

"10 o'clock this morning."

"You must be joking."

"I'm not. Johnson wants it so it looks like tha'll have to go on t' bus or use the car, which nobody ever seems to want to drive."

Alan groaned. He had planned to be at Drax before 11am because he had a couple of people there to see first, though that was more for social rather than any technical reasons. Nothing he could do about that though, and so he had to go to Mick's office, get the keys for the car, drive it next to the van and load it up. By the time he had reached the M62, it was well turned nine.

He had aimed to get past Ferrybridge Power Station by half 10 and as he went past Milnrow he thought that he would do. But due to heavy traffic, he had to drive very slowly for the next 20 miles. As a result, he did not get past the cooling towers at Ferrybridge before 11.30 and it was well after 12 before he pulled into Drax car park.

He pushed the trolley into reception and asked the girl on the desk to phone his contact, Eddie. Twenty minutes later he arrived, having just finished his dinner. He was quite surprised to see Alan, and wondered why he had come all the way from darkest Lancashire. Had nobody told him that the job he had come to do had been cancelled? Mr Johnson had been informed the previous week. Eddie himself had rung him and told him.

There was nothing he could do other than leave the trolley in reception while he went and had his dinner. On the way back, he thought about calling in at Ferrybridge, but decided against it as the traffic going westbound was very heavy. It was well after five before he arrived back at work. The van was in the same place it had been before. One thing Alan had noticed some nine hours earlier was the mileage. It was exactly 66,000. Now it read 66,012. Wherever Mr Johnson had driven it was just six miles away.

He went into Mick's office. He was there talking to one of his drivers who had just returned from his journey to Eggborough Power Station. As soon as he had gone, Alan told Mick that the car needed a new clutch; it had left a pool of oil on Drax car park and the brakes needed urgent attention too. In his view the car was on its last legs.

"Don't you mean its last wheels?"

"Whatever it's on, I am not driving it again. Anyway, where has the van been today? It's only done 12 miles since this morning."

What had happened was that Mr Johnson had walked into Mick's office in the middle of the morning and asked for the keys. As he did so, the phone had rung for him. While he was on the phone, Mick had nipped down to the van to find out just what the boss had put in it.

"Just making sure the jack was there" Mick had lied when Mr Johnson asked where he had just been. What Mick had actually found out was the destination of the box and maybe why the boss had not used the company's usual means of dispatching its products.

"So where was the box going to, Mick?"

"Devon."

"Mary Tavy Power Station, I presume."

"No, to a hotel in Barnstaple, which seems a bit of a funny place to send high voltage electrical control gear."

When he finally arrived home at well after six, Thelma had two bits of news for him and a reminder that they were going to see their friends Joyce and Sam after tea. Joyce had rung up earlier in the day to remind Thelma just in case she had forgotten, but she hadn't.

The first bit of news was that their son Robert had phoned to say that he would not be calling on Saturday, because he had arranged to go with a few mates on an anti-war demonstration in London. By now the news coming out of America was really disturbing. George Bush and Dick Cheney were increasingly pushing for an invasion of Iraq and

Tony Blair appeared keen for Britain to be involved. Few members of the Labour Government were prepared to oppose him, hence the need for a large national demonstration to show how much public opposition there was in the country to the war-mongers' plans.

The second bit of news was about the house on the opposite side of the street which was up for sale. That afternoon a car had pulled up and out of it had stepped a man who Thelma was sure was the Saints half-back Tommy Martyn. She thought that he lived in Leigh, but maybe he was thinking of going upmarket. After all, that is what a move from Leigh to Ashurst many people might consider to be.

Thelma drove them up to Gillarsfield where Joyce had lived most of her life. Sam had been there since 1947 after he left the Merchant Navy, married her and three months later started work at Wilkinson's. He was now 83; Joyce would soon be 78. Sam looked it, though Joyce didn't, except for the fact that her permanent companion, which had once been a little dog, was now a walking stick. Both though were still mentally active, which was shown by the number of books covering a wide range of topics in a large bookcase. Also on a table was a chessboard with a game still in progress.

Their first topic of conversation was about what various members of their families were doing, but it soon moved on to matters of wider interest. The current policies of the Labour Government came in for a lot of criticism; nothing new there. Thelma worked in the local Oxfam shop two days a week and spoke about various things she had heard from her customers.

Then Alan told Joyce and Sam how their son Robert had recently become involved in the Ashurst Stop the War Coalition. His interest in the politics of the Middle East had started a few years earlier when he had been at Coventry University; but since then, he hadn't been involved in anything remotely political. But now he was going to take part in the anti-war demonstration in London at the weekend.

"Good for him. I'd go myself if I could do. I've been watching this situation over Iraq develop with some interest. Dick Cheney wants war, Bush is being a little less bullish but it's clear that's what he wants too. I'm just waiting to see not if, but when, Tony Blair gets into bed with them. What none of these politicians seem to understand is that if the West does invade Iraq, it will only make the whole situation in the Middle East much worse than it is now."

This was what Alan would have expected Sam to say. Over the years Sam had often talked at work about his own experiences in the Second World War. Other older colleagues had also often spoken about what they had done between 1939 and 1945. They were interesting and educational for the younger draughtsmen, some of whom had later done their National Service, but not Alan. By the time he had finished his apprenticeship, it had finished.

At this point Sam excused himself to pay a call and while he was out of the room, Thelma asked Joyce how he was.

"He's not too bad. A bit forgetful, hardly ever goes much further than the bottom of the garden and often nods off in his chair, but then he is 83. I have to say though that when I told him that you two were coming round tonight, he perked up no end."

"We'll have to come more often then."

"Please do. It's the same when Paul or Maureen or any of the grandchildren come, as long as they don't stay too long."

"Is that a hint that we should be leaving now?"

"No, not at all. You stay as long as you want and I mean that."

Sam returned, sat down, took a gulp from his glass, turned to Joyce and with a smile on his face asked: "Have you all been talking about me, while I've been gone eh?"

"I've just been telling them how you enjoy friends and relatives calling round to see you and Thelma said they might arrange to come and see you again next year or maybe the year after."

Sam laughed and asked whether it was Timbuktoo where they were living now and then before Thelma or Alan could think of a suitable reply, he said: "Do you know Thelma, I can still remember the very first time I ever saw you at work."

They waited as he brushed his lips with the back of his hand and went on: "I were in the Print Room with Mick, Mick Henderson you know, the lad from Platt Bridge in Wigan. Alan were in there too with Keith Sanderson, probably talking about rugby. Big Joan came in with you and said 'You lads are going to have to behave when you come in here now. We've got a lady with us'. And Alan said 'Well she'll be the first one they've had in here for a long time.'

"And then for the next few weeks I often saw him talking to you and I thought to myself, I bet he's going to ask her for a date and then when we all came back after Christmas he told us what had happened and how you were living at his granny's. And look where you are now, still stuck with him."

"Nice glue though. Must be the same one you used."

"Do you know what we used to call you when you first started; Freckles was one of your nicknames and another was Ban the Bomb because of that shoulder bag you always carried round with you, the one with that CND badge on the side. I can see that you have still got your freckles. Have you still got that bag?"

"I have Sam, and I'll tell you what, I'll bring it with me when we come again which will probably be sometime next year."

"What day will it be and what time? I'll have the kettle on for you."

"I'll get back to you on that one, but you'd better remind me."

Sam laughed. "That is what Grovesy used to say. I wonder where he is now. Didn't he run off to Spain with that blonde woman who used to work in the gas showrooms in Warrington, the one that looked like Marilyn Monroe?"

The phone rang. It was for Sam, so he went into the front room, saying as he left the room, that if it was Percy from Selby he would probably be away for a couple of hours.

"So Joyce, how did you two get to know each other? I've often wondered."

"It was all thanks to my cousin, Norman. He was on the same ship as Sam, and when he got married he invited Sam and a few other members of the crew to the wedding, but only Sam turned up. After the ceremony was over, we all went to the reception in St John's Church Hall. At the time I was a war widow with my son, Paul. Norman introduced us and we started chatting and got on very well. He said that he was thinking of leaving the Merchant Navy, getting a job as an electrician and settling down somewhere.

"I asked him would it be in Halifax and he said no. It might be round here, the people all seem nice and as he said that, he looked me in the eyes and gave me a little kiss on the cheek. It was so romantic I thought and then Paul started pulling at my frock asking if we could go home because he was fed up and wanted to play out. I could have killed him, well you know what I mean, and then Sam said would I like him to walk us home as he could do with some fresh air and didn't really know anybody in the room.

"We came back here and he was so easy to talk with. I invited him in, he played with Paul for a bit, then he looked at the clock on the mantelpiece and my heart fell. I was sure he was going to leave and that I'd never see him again.

"He put his coat on and as he did he asked if he could write to me. He still had another six months to do in the Merchant Navy and didn't know when he would be back in England again. I gave him my address, he kissed me again and then he left. A week later I got a letter and an address to write to, if I wanted to. A few weeks later he sent me a couple of photos of him taken in Port Said and I sent him some of me and Paul. I had a few more letters from him from different places and then I got one telling me that he was in a hospital in Liverpool recovering from some illness he had picked up in west Africa. Not long after that his contract finished. Within a month he had got a job in Wigan and soon after we got married and that was the happiest day of my life."

At that point Sam reappeared looking rather sad. The call he had just taken was from another old shipmate telling him that Percy had been in a road accident and was now in a hospital in Pontefract. By now it had turned 10 o'clock and time for Thelma and Alan to leave.

"Thanks for coming you two," Joyce said as she walked to the car with them. "I can tell how much he's enjoyed you being here. He'll be fine for a couple of weeks now. The first thing that'll happen is we will finish that game of chess game. Then he'll write a couple of letters to some of his old pals, ask me to go to the library with him and he'll be just like he was when he was still working."

She continued: "I forget to ask but how's Charlie going on? Sam keeps saying that he'll have to go up to Thatto Heath to see him sometime, but I don't think he ever will. They were two good mates them two, they really were."

"We'll come again in a couple of weeks" said Thelma "and I think we are going up to see Charlie soon as well so maybe we'll arrange to bring him here with us. Anyway we'll pass on your best wishes and it's been lovely to see you both."

And with that she hugged Joyce and as she did so she felt sad. Sam was so different from how Thelma had first known him and she felt he would not be with them for much longer. She felt sorry for Joyce too, for she and Sam had been such a nice pair of people to have as friends. But then, when people turn 80 they could be considered as being on borrowed time, but as it turned out neither Sam or Joyce were ready to depart from Planet Earth just yet.

Back home they watched *BBC News* and *Newsnight.* Parliament had been recalled that day to discuss the contents of a dossier that had been produced by the Joint Intelligence Committee. It alleged that Iraq had reconstituted its nuclear weapons programme and possessed chemical and biological weapons of mass destruction, some of which could be ready to fire in 45 minutes. But where were these weapons located and how and when had they been assembled? There was no clear evidence to prove their existence, but despite that, the government was acting as though there was. The pro-war view was growing in momentum on the other side of the Atlantic too. For a long time Saddam Hussein had been the West's ally in the Middle East which explained why successive British governments had once been encouraged to sell millions of pounds worth of armaments to him.

Now those same weapons might well be used against any invading forces, British, American or whoever else they might include. The best course of action to prevent this happening would be to allow more time for weapons inspectors to continue to try and find them. But would the White House allow any time for that? It was increasingly unlikely. And who would ever believe Tony Blair, who now appeared to many people to want to take the country to war based on the existence and threat from weapons that may not even exist.

Certainly not Sam or Joyce Holroyd, not Alan or Thelma or Robert Greenall either; although their daughter Rebecca might just have a slightly different view on the matter.

5. Listening to Eddie and Stevo

The next morning Alan was in work early again. He had a busy day in front of him. The first thing he had to do was talk to Cliff about the design of a water treatment plant at Calabozo in Venezuela. Then he had to ring Tony Griffiths, who had hopefully by now arrived at a cotton mill in Milan. He had to spend some time with Mr Johnson to put him in the picture about problems in the Meter Room at Mary Tavy, something that would probably mean him having to make a site visit and by half four he had to be at the dentist's. No matter what happened then, by seven o'clock he had to be in Victoria Park playing for the Eccleston Arms in the Ashurst Crown Green Bowls League Division Four game against Gillarsfield Conservative Club 'B' team.

That was the plan, but as usual things didn't quite work out that way. Cliff rang to tell him that he had forgotten to mention that he had a hospital appointment that morning. His conversation with Tony Griffiths lasted just five minutes and then Mr Johnson's secretary told him that his meeting with the boss was off. He was now on his way to Manchester Airport to catch the next flight to Amsterdam for yet another meeting.

The following morning Alan was in early again. The first thing he had to do was to ring the cotton mill at Accrington, which was where he was intending to go to sort out their chute feed system. But his conversation with the works engineer was short, just long enough for Maurice to tell him that a decision had just been made to close the place with immediate effect and so the next time anybody would need to come from Ashurst would be to remove machinery and not to try to find out why it wasn't working.

He made two more phone calls, read a report of Colin's recent visit to Eggborough Power Station and was then interrupted by the man himself waving a large piece of paper.

"Morning, boss. Are you on six-two this week?"

"No, I came in early to get a few things sorted out before I went to Accrington, but I'm not going now. I've just been told they're closing the place."

"So, no more lunchtime soirees with Accrington Sally?"

Sally was the barmaid in the pub Alan always ate at when he was in East Lancashire.

"Only if I have to go up there to get our machines dismantled."

"So you're not in a good mood then. Well I don't suppose it will be any use me asking you to read and sign this highly important document."

"What is it?"

"It's a petition. A bit like the petition for that campaign that stopped Lord Beeching closing Ashurst Railway Station, the one that you once played some insignificant role in back in the year dot."

Colin put a piece of paper on Alan's desk and waited for his reaction to what was written on it.

"We, the undersigned residents of Ashurst, oppose the decision by the Council to remove the Mount Geronimo slag heap on the grounds of health and safety."

"Who has organised this?"

"Gillarsfield Residents Association."

"And I suppose you are on their committee?"

"Yes, but don't worry. It isn't a full-time post. Well, not yet, so I'll keep coming here every day, until I can find a good enough reason to not keep coming here every day."

Where else had anybody organised a campaign to keep a slag heap in existence? But then, Mount Geronimo was no ordinary slag heap. If ever there had been a competition for the most beautiful bit of industrial wasteland in Lancashire, the Geronimo would surely have won it. Trees which attracted a fascinating collection of birds had grown on it; daffodils, tulips and roses had grown on it; potatoes, leeks and carrots could be found there too. In 1948, it had even been the venue for the Lancashire Stonies World Cup!

At one end was a lake where fish swam in warm water throughout the year; the heat came from the smouldering spontaneous combustion of sulphur and coal that lay below it in abundance. Over the years the wooded area had been quite a romantic spot too and, although they would never know it, many local children had probably been conceived on it too.

For years though it had been dwarfed by its neighbour, Mount Everest. Now all evidence of its existence had gone, all as a result of intense activity by the local Council which had turned it into the site of the West Bold housing estate. On a very clear day it was possible to stand on the top of the Geronimo and see the Wigan Alps, near to where Jennifer now lived. Looking south, the cooling towers of Fiddlers Ferry Power Station could also be seen with their distinctive cloud formations rising over the scenic ancient village of Widnes.

Many tales could be told about things that had happened on the Geronimo over the years. Some were humorous; some were sad and some were almost unbelievable. One had involved his own grandfather, quite a moving tale too. It had been 1926 when the Ashurst miners were still on strike. He had gone out early one Sunday morning to scavenge for coal. It was freezing in their house and there were children there to try and keep warm. He had spent over an hour collecting slack, bits of wood and anything else that might burn, when a policeman appeared on the scene. He told him that what he had put in his sack was 'stolen property' and had given him just one minute to empty it out on the ground, otherwise he would arrest him.

Alan signed Colin's petition and as he did he remembered the 1962 petition to save Ashurst Railway Station and the branch line to Leigh He remembered going round the town to ask people for their support.

There had been a few other good things too that had resulted from his involvement in that campaign. He had met a few old friends from Lane Head Junior School, the drummer from Bill Unsworth's band at the Wigan Emp Dancehall, three famous rugby players and Phil Bond, with whom he had been in the same night school class as at Ashurst Technical College, when they were both studying for their HNC in Electrical Engineering.

There was a 'Sold' sign outside the house where they had met. It had belonged to Phil's late father. Phil was there clearing things out when Alan had knocked on the front door. He told Alan about his father's recent death and to have a walk round the house and if he saw anything that he wanted, he could take it because on Saturday morning, everything that was left was going in a skip. Phil's wife was expecting and he had neither the time nor patience to go through what was still there. That evening Alan didn't collect any more signatures, but he did get quite a lot of interesting old newspapers, magazines and comics.

At the age of 63, Alan didn't think he could now whip up much enthusiasm to join Colin in his campaign to keep a slag heap open. He doubted it, although he did know he would miss the old place if it did disappear. He had spent many happy hours playing there when he was young. It was the place where he had tried smoking his first cigarette along with four other lads. Just as he was taking his first drag, his sister Joan had arrived to tell him that his tea was ready. By the time he had arrived home, she had already told his mother. She had given him a good slap on his leg, told him never to do that again and, as a result, he had never held a cigarette in his hand again.

Colin was a Wiganer, although he now lived at Nook End. On the very day that he had been born in 1962, the house that his parents would once have loved to have taken him home to near Shevington was being demolished to make way for the building of the M6 motorway. Because of this, his parents had been moved to a council house in Platt Bridge where Colin lived until he married a girl from Newton-le-Willows and bought a house at Nook End. Colin had never mentioned any of this until a few days ago during a lunchtime conversation about things they could remember doing as small boys. It had come to light that one of Colin's former neighbours had been their old workmate Mick Henderson, who had died 10 years earlier.

A few days later Colin came into work with a bit of news about Mick's widow, Elizabeth. On visiting his mother, who still lived in their old house, Colin had asked about her and discovered that she had recently gone to live with her daughter at Goose Green. Now there was a new family living there. It was Mr and Mrs Popadovolitch or something like that. Quite a nice couple too and certainly much nicer than the family on the other side of the house, whose flock included four unruly children and two large Alsatian dogs.

The new occupants were quite an educated family too, particularly if their eldest child Anton was anything to go by. Although he was only eight years old, the lad could already hold conversations in both English and Polish.

By now it was early October and what some people liked to call the business end of the rugby league season. The Saints' next game was against the Bradford Bulls in the Super League Qualifying semi-final. Whoever won this game would be in the Grand Final in a fortnight's time. He and Thelma, along with their neighbour Phil, set off, hoping for a win. At half-time, they all feared the worst, because the Yorkshiremen went into the dressing rooms winning 26–4. But despite the Saints pulling out all the stops in the second half, they were still not quite good enough and the Bulls won 28–26. Now the Saints had to beat Colin's team from the other side of Billinge in the Elimination semi-final in order to face Bradford again at Old Trafford.

First thing on the Monday morning, Mr Johnson walked into Alan's office with the expected request for him to go to the Hydroelectric Power Station at Mary Tavy in Devon. Alan decided to go by train. He didn't fancy driving all the way there for something that might take little more than a morning to sort out and then have to drive all the way back the next day. That was what Mr Johnson would have liked him to do, and probably in the death trap that was the work's car as well; but Alan no longer enjoyed long distance driving.

Luckily he had made the right decision. The weather turned bad on the day he would have been driving there and there had been long hold-ups on both the M6 and the M5. Sitting on the train, and in a first class carriage too, was the way to travel, particularly when he started chatting to a Portuguese couple who had once lived in the city of Porto. They were both lecturers at Liverpool University, lived in Maghull, and had as near neighbours the parents of a young man beginning to make a name for himself at Knowsley Road, James Graham.

When Alan arrived at the power station, he was pleased to discover that the man in charge was an old friend. It was John Smith, an engineer who had once worked for the Central Electricity Generating Board when they had their offices in the centre of Leeds. John now lived in the nearby town of Tavistock, but as soon as he started talking it was clear by the way that he pronounced the letter T, that he still sounded like someone from the Heavy Woollen District.

During lunch, John told Alan that a few months earlier his daughter had paid for a year's subscription to Sky Sports for his 60th birthday present. As a result he had been able to start watching Super League games every Friday night. The third week he had invited his neighbour to watch the game with him. Stanley really enjoyed it and so John told him that he was welcome to watch it every week; well, they were good neighbours. A couple of weeks later, they were joined by another neighbour, Ronald, a former welder in a Barrow shipyard, and once a friend of the international player Willie Horne.

The room in which John had his TV was quite large, well now it had to be, because soon after two more of the regulars from their local heard about what was being shown every Friday night and before long rugby league had four new supporters and John's front room had four regular Friday night visitors.

One person who was unhappy about this new arrangement was the landlord of their local, so much so that, despite his reluctance, he was forced into showing rugby league games whenever they were on Sky, in the main room. Another person who was not very pleased with this was Cecil, one of the regulars. Many years ago, he had played rugby union for the county, a fact he somehow managed to make known every time he was sat in there. Cecil had no objection to professional football, darts, cricket, snooker or American football being shown in what had been his local ever since he was 18 years old, but the one thing he just could not stand was anything to do with that old Northern Union stuff polluting the West Country atmosphere and getting a foothold in the area.

So now John was able to watch his favourite sport with all the locals and then go home and watch the recording whenever he wanted. That was the way to stop his front room becoming more like a room in a public house, which had become rather upsetting for his dear wife Margaret.

Despite being invited to stay and watch Friday's game, there was no way Alan was going to miss being on the terraces at Knowsley Road for the clash with Wigan in the Elimination semi-final. The game looked like being a cracker and two days later it was, with the Saints winning 24–8 in front of over 15,000 spectators.

John could understood why Alan did not want to stay any longer than was absolutely necessary and made sure that he got away in good time. There were other technical problems that needed attention in the meter room, but they could wait for a few weeks until after the season had finished and when it would be more convenient for Alan to return.

As a result he was on the first train out of Exeter on the Thursday morning. John had driven him there and on the way had told him that one of the things he loved about watching the game on Sky was listening to the two commentators, Mike Stevenson and Eddie Hemmings.

"Stevo is an old mate of mine. I knew him from when we were

both at Victoria Secondary Modern in Dewsbury. If you ever see him on your travels, give him my regards and ask him if he still remembers that time we all went to our kid's stag do in Cleckheaton. He'll remember it. I know he will. Hilarious it was. Tell him that I've still got the scars to prove it."

And then he added: "And if they ever have any games down here and he comes to commentate on them, tell him that he can kip on the settee in our front room if he ever wants to."

6. "I hate this bloody war"

Alan got off the train at Warrington Bank Quay station and caught a taxi home. As it drove into Silkstone Street, he glanced at the front of his house and his heart almost stopped beating. All the curtains were drawn and yet it was only five o'clock in the afternoon. Had Thelma or Rebecca or Robert died? Maybe it was his brother Paul who had been in hospital recently. Then he saw that many other houses in the street also had their curtains closed. Hopefully it might just be the traditional mark of respect for a neighbour because the street had more than its fair share of older residents.

As he walked through the front door, he saw Thelma coming down the stairs. She looked her usual happy-go-lucky self, so it clearly wasn't her or either of their children or his brother.

"What's happened? Who's died?"

"Mrs Higham on Wednesday."

Ever since she had moved into the street in 1921, Mrs Higham had been a good friend of Alan's grandmother. At the beginning of the year, she had gone to live in the Greenfield Old Peoples' Home in Dob Lane and now she had sadly passed away.

"What a relief. I nearly had a heart attack when I saw all the curtains were drawn."

He unpacked his suitcase while Thelma made a pot of tea, and then told him what else had happened in Ashurst while he had been away and he told her about meeting his old friend John Smith. Then she returned to the death of Mrs Higham: "The funeral is next Thursday at St Luke's. I'll be going, your Joan is as well, but your Paul won't be. He's still not well enough yet. Do you think you'll able to get time off work for it?"

Mrs Higham was a lovely old lady, similar to his grandmother in so many ways. Her husband had been a collier all his life and had been killed underground at the Prince of Wales in 1947 a few weeks after the country's coal mines had been brought together into the National Coal Board, an organisation which now no longer existed. She had raised three children. Her eldest son had been killed in the War in North Africa and her second had gone to work in Preston in the early 1950s, but had always kept in regular contact with his mother. The youngest still lived in Ashurst, had never done anything much with his life, and could never find the time to visit her.

Thelma went on to tell him that Joyce had rung and suggested that they went up to see her and Sam as soon as Alan was back and she had arranged for them to go up tonight.

While he had been away, it had been announced that a team of United Nations arms inspectors was returning to Iraq to see if they could find any evidence of the alleged weapons of mass destruction. Other inspectors had spent time looking and found nothing, so hopefully this could mean that the chance of war breaking out in the Middle East might be prevented, or at least delayed until a more peaceful solution could be found.

As he walked through reception the following morning, he was met by Mr Johnson who wanted to know in detail how successful his visit to Mary Tavy had been, and so it was nearly 10 o'clock before he was back in the Drawing Office. He had a long discussion with Cliff about what had happened in his absence and how he might have to go down to the West Country again quite soon.

"All this travelling and sleeping in strange beds, you just don't know how tough it is at the top, Cliff."

"Not half as tough as it is at the top of Billinge," muttered Cliff, who was now having loads of aggro with his new neighbours, their teenage daughter Zoe and her bunch of Boy George lookalike friends.

"I suppose you all missed me while I was away."

"I did, but only once. When are you going away again?"

"Thursday next week, to a funeral, so you can all look forward to another day enjoying the golden art of idleness."

With that, he went up to the top end of the office and spent half an hour with Graham Healey, a mechanical engineer who was working on a quite complicated job for Didcot Power Station.

The following week was taken up by meetings with Mr Johnson and endless telephone calls with electricians and fitters working on site all over the place. Most of the Friday morning was taken with a fruitless discussion with Mr Johnson about office efficiency and good housekeeping and so by the time he had a few minutes to himself, it was time to go to the Eagle and Child for their regular Friday lunchtime drink.

There Alan talked about what had happened at the funeral and about a conversation he had had with one of the mourners.

After Mrs Higham had been buried, the mourners had all gone to the Edinburgh cafe in Bridge Street. There Alan had met an old man who he did not know. It was someone who had news from the past of great interest to both him and his sister Joan.

"Are you three Mrs Holding's grandchildren then?" was his opening question as they all sat down, waiting for the meal to be served. Joan told him that she and Alan were, but Thelma was Alan's wife and his brother Paul was still recovering from an operation he had recently had in Victoria Hospital.

"Well, I don't suppose that you will know who I am."

They sat there silently as he continued: "Mrs Higham was my auntie, which is why I am here and why I know a lot about you two."

His comment came as a surprise so they said nothing and allowed him to carry on: "I grew up on Billinge Road opposite the Wigan Arms, not far from Hamer Street where your dad used to live. He was a pal of my older brother Frank. Shortly after the war started the pair of them joined up, just before Christmas it was. At the time I was in Whiston Isolation Hospital with scarlet fever. It was quite common in them days. So it was around the middle of 1940 before I was able to join the Army. In fact, my first week coincided with the evacuation from Dunkirk. A bad time it was; we survived, but only just. A couple of years later, I found myself in Italy fighting our way up from Sicily. That's when I lost my arm, at Monte Casino."

He nodded down to his left hand side where his sleeve was pinned to a jacket which had clearly seen better days.

"They took me to a field hospital a few miles back. They put me in a bed and when I turned to see who was next to me, I recognised your dad straightaway. We had plenty to talk about, where we had been, what we had done over the last couple of years and what had happened to our Frank and a couple of other lads we both knew.

"He told me all about his family, his three fine children, his lovely wife and your house in Chisnall Avenue. He showed me some photographs he had of you and one of them was taken in Silkstone Street. That's how I discovered that your grandmother was Mrs Holding and a friend of my auntie Elsie. He went on and on about what you three were like and how he hated this bloody war. I could tell he was suffering and maybe talking to someone from his own background was a big help to him.

"I think that he was the first bloke from Ashurst I had been with since 1940. I really enjoyed hearing someone talking with an Ashurst accent again, but I could see he was in a bad way. The nurse used to come almost every hour to change his dressings and feed him. After a couple of weeks, they took him down to the operating theatre again. He must have already been three or four times while I was there.

"Just before he went he gave me some photographs to look at again. I think he must have known he might not be coming back. I fell asleep and when I woke up the nurse told me he had died.

"'What a bloody awful war this is.' That's what he used to say and he was right. All he ever wanted to do was to be back home in Ashurst with his wife and his children and working at his old job on the shop floor in Mather's Foundry."

He paused for breath and then went on: "I've still got the photographs he gave me at home. I've kept them all these years. If you let me have your address I'll post them to you. There's a couple of letters too from your mum. Is she still alive? What's her name?"

"No, she died in 1979. Her name was Doreen."

"Yes, that's it. I remember now. There's some photographs of her and one of your granny and granddad as well. I suppose they all be dead now, won't they?"

He told them that his name was Ronald Higham and he lived with his sister in Bedford, hastening to add that it was Bedford in Leigh and not Bedford down south. Then to take his mind off what had obviously been a bad time in his life, he changed the subject: "Are you a rugby man then" and assuming Alan must be, he went on: "Who do you follow?"

"The Saints" said Thelma.

He looked at her in amazement as if a woman following rugby league was quite unusual. Well, maybe it might have been when he had first started going to the match. It certainly wasn't now though. It wasn't even unusual when Thelma had first visited Knowsley Road for that game against Oldham in 1963. But maybe 30 years earlier in 1933 it might have been.

"I haven't seen a game for years. You see after the war I married a nurse from Dover, so I went living down in Kent with her. I never liked it there though, there was no rugby for a start, but what chance did a one armed fitter have?"

43

Before he could tell them how he had earned his living, and what had made him come back to Leigh, another man sat nearby pointed to his watch and told Ronald that it was time for them to be going.

Alan wrote his address on a scrap of paper and as he gave it to Ronald, Thelma asked if it would be better if they came to Leigh to collect them. He agreed; that was much easier than him having to traipse down to the Post Office to buy the stamps.

It was a good job Thelma had suggested that. They went to see him on the following Saturday morning only to discover that he had been taken into the Royal Bolton Hospital the previous day. His sister was now keen to get rid of as much of his stuff as possible while he was out of the way and so they came away with a fascinating amount of historical memorabilia. As Alan looked through what they had been given later, he realised that he might be able to use some of it in a novel that he had been thinking of writing for some time.

And so it was to prove because what he now had in his possession did not just refer to the life and times of Ronald Higham, interesting though that was. The material covered details of Ronald's father who had been brought up on a farm in Rainford and an auntie Alice who had played football with Dick Kerr's Ladies alongside the famous Lily Parr who came from Gerard's Bridge in St Helens. Everything was packed in large envelopes with their contents labelled on white stickers. The first they opened had the title "Muck Stacks".

In it they found a collection of photographs, all neatly packaged together. There were seven photographs in the first group, each with details written on the back. In his earlier conversation with them, Ronald had also spoken of how he had lived in the small Yorkshire mining town of Featherstone for a time. A lot of the photographs were evidence of this and included some of various slag heaps around the town, or muck stacks as they are called in that part of the world.

It was obvious that Ronald had been very interested in the mining industry. There were photos of seven pits in the area, including Sharlston, Ackton Hall, Featherstone Main and Allerton Bywater.

There were also a few photographs of a well-dressed lady. One was titled 'Theresa in Bridlington', another 'Theresa on Station Road'. However, they were never to know who she was because a week later Ronald's sister rang to tell them that her brother had passed away following an operation in the hospital and would be buried in Leigh

Cemetery the following day.

She went on to say that she was now intending to go and live on the Isle of Man with her sister as soon as she could sell her house. She would be more than happy for Alan to have any of Ronald's stuff that he wanted; otherwise it was all going to a charity shop in Leigh, along with all her furniture. She didn't want any money for it. She just wanted to get shut of it all.

As a result, Alan took his son Robert round the following week, loaded up as much as the van they had hired would hold and drove it to Latchford, where Robert had just put down a deposit to rent a flat.

Alan was more than pleased a few days later when, in the act of trying to retrieve a pound coin that had slipped out of his pocket down the side of the settee, he had found a medal from the Crimean War. Knowing that Robert was going to get rid of the settee as soon as possible because of its awful smell, Alan had cut away the underside cover and exposed an assortment of newspapers.

The first paper he read included an account of the opening of Ashurst Railway Station in 1882 and the death of a priest at St Theresa's Church. He had been hit by a wagon in the railway goods yard. It was an interesting story because there was absolutely no reason for him to have been there.

Flicking through the papers, he saw many other interesting stories from much further afield. They included an account of the ending of the Second Anglo-Afghan War in 1880 and the start of first Anglo-Boer War in the same year, British troops occupying Alexandria and the Suez Canal, the founding of the Boys Brigade by Sir William Smith, the first telephone directory containing just 248 entries, the publication of *Treasure Island* by Robert Louis Stevenson and the deaths of both Charles Darwin and Karl Marx.

He didn't stay long there with Robert because he now had to go and visit Tony Griffiths. He lived fairly near, at Stockton Heath. After Tony had returned from the Far East, it had been his plan to spend all his time based in the factory, either in the Wiring Shop or with the Maintenance Department. But as things had turned out his skills had soon been needed first in Slovenia and then at Rugeley Power Station in Staffordshire. As a result, the pair of them had not had any chance to get together, something that Tony wanted because there was something he wanted to discuss with Alan.

45

This was the first time Alan had been to Tony's house and he was in for a bit of a surprise when he knocked on the front door 10 minutes after leaving Robert's flat.

It was opened by young, good looking woman of Far Eastern appearance. Well, she was a bit more than that; she was nothing less than an outstanding beauty. Alan knew that the one thing that had kept Tony and his wife Marjorie together over the years had been the fact that he had spent most of his time out of her sight working abroad. The more they were apart it would seem, the longer their marriage would last. Now that he had decided he was going to spend the rest of his working life, living at home, had she left him? So who was this young beauty? Was it Marjorie's replacement? Was she someone Tony had got to know during the time he had spent in Thailand?

That might have been the case, knowing Tony as well as Alan did, but it wasn't. As soon as the woman began to speak, it was clear that her English was perfect, well as perfect as it could be for someone who had grown up in a house on Penny Lane a few miles away in Liverpool. Nor was she in a relationship with Tony. She was the girlfriend of his son Andy, who from time-to-time lived there whenever his job as a soldier in the British Army would allow it.

7. Hazel says 'no' to Bush and Blair

It was 19 October, the day of the Grand Final between the Saints and the Bradford Bulls at Old Trafford. Alan had arranged to go with Dave Frodsham who lived a couple of miles away at Nook End. He stood outside the house at half four, and chatted to one of his neighbours, Dennis, who was also going, in his case with his son who lived at Haresfinch. If Alan had known, they could all have gone in the same car. Minutes later a car with a Saints flag sticking out of the window drove past, but it was not Dave, although the face of the driver was familiar, probably someone who drank in the Ring o' Bells.

By quarter to five there was no sign of Dave. He asked Thelma to ring him. No answer. She rang again. No answer. He waited a bit longer and a bit longer by which time it had become too late to go. There was nothing he could do because Dave had the tickets anyway. He would have to watch the game on the big screen in his local.

A lot of people now preferred to watch the game in the pub. You could see more that way; the best of the action was played three or four times from different angles and at slower speeds. Maybe it was not as good as being at the ground where you could enjoy the atmosphere, but that was not always true. It was certainly not true at Odsal Stadium when it was raining and you were standing a long way from the pitch. Then it was much better to be in the pub. There you also had the choice to stand up or sit down, not like at many of the new grounds where you had to sit and stand depending on what the people in front of you were doing.

It was a good game to watch, particularly for all the Saints fans because they won, but only just, 19–18, in front of over 61,000 spectators. As soon as the final whistle had gone, a few people left to go elsewhere. As Alan was stood at the bar, a man walked up to him, stuck out his hand and said: "Hallo Alan. How are you?"

It was Keith Tabern who had been Alan's neighbour when the Greenalls had lived in Beswick Street. Keith had once worked at Wilkinson's in the Machine Shop, but along with many others, he had been made redundant in 1999, since when they had not met.

Alan had not intended staying much longer in the pub, but there was plenty for them to talk about, so much so that he was one of the last people to leave the place.

The following Monday morning he left for work at half seven as usual. Soon he was back home, packing his suitcase. Mr Johnson had phoned him as soon as he had arrived with an urgent request for him to go to the Rosario Cotton Mill in Portugal. None of the four machines they had recently installed were working and they just had to be up and running by the end of the week or there would not be any more orders placed by the company.

When Alan arrived at the mill the following day three of the machines were running. The problem with each had been the same, which the mill electrician had finally discovered. The problem with the fourth was a bit more complicated and so it was late on Thursday before he was back in Ashurst.

"Well, Mrs Greenall, what has been happening in Ashurst while I've been away? Have you done anything exciting or been anywhere that you can tell me about?"

"On Monday night I went to Ashurst Library."

"Wow, that must have been really good."

"It was. Do you remember Mrs Hunter, who was involved in that campaign with us to stop the Council closing Bell Lane Library?

"Yes."

"Well I went with Joyce to listen to her talk about her recent holiday in the Arctic Circle. There were over 50 people there and she wasn't the slightest bit nervous. Not like she used to be."

"And what else can you tell me about this week?"

"Your friend Hazel has been upsetting a few people in town."

"Why? What has she done now?"

"You know that she and three teachers at her school all joined the Labour Party a few months ago."

"Yes, I did know, although I was disappointed when I heard about it. I always thought she was a socialist."

"Well, while you've been away, there has been a lot more on the television about Iraq's alleged weapons of mass destruction. That Dutchman Hans Blix has been in contact with various members of the American government, who don't all seem to be telling the same story. George Bush has said he is prepared to go along with the United Nations, but at the same time he is not prepared to wait much longer. In other words, if they don't agree to what he wants, he'll ignore them.

"Then on *Newsnight* last night there was somebody from the government on, claiming there were over 10,000 litres of Anthrax in Iraq still unaccounted for since 1991. But that was challenged by a scientist who said that the shelf life of liquid Anthrax was no more than three years and so what they had would be useless by now.

"It's clear that Blair wants us to go to war. He's forever stressing what a violent dictator Saddam is. But he hasn't changed that much since he was our ally and we were selling him weapons, chemicals and probably Anthrax too. Another thing is that the Americans are trying to link Saddam with Al-Qaeda but they don't have any evidence to prove it. I think that it is just a case of Bush and Cheney wanting an excuse for going to war with someone who they don't like."

"That wouldn't be the first time."

"Yes, I know. But the problem for them is that they don't want to go it alone. They need allies and that's why George Bush desperately wants Tony Blair to show that he is full agreement with him."

"I know all that, but what has it got to do with Hazel?"

"Last week she told a friend who is a journalist from the *Ashurst Star* that if Blair takes this country into a war, she will resign from the Labour Party and she'll take at least six other members with her. She also said that there are more Labour Party members in Ashurst who have said that they will leave if anything Blair agrees to does not have the full support of the United Nations. The journalist made a great story out of it and they have put on the front page too."

"Well done, Hazel. I agree completely with her. In fact I think I'll do the same."

"Alan, you can't resign from an organisation that that you are not even a member of."

"Well, put it this way, if I were a member of the Labour Party I would resign from it too."

Then he continued: "One thing that Hans Blix might find if he looks very carefully in Iraq might be a load of our drawings."

"What do you mean?"

"In 1991 we designed a mechanical handling and weighing system for a chemical plant in Germany. We found out later that it was actually for a chemical plant that a German company was building in Iraq. They had subcontracted some of the work to us, because they didn't have the capacity to do it in their own premises. That was at a time when the Tory government was very friendly with Saddam Hussein, and selling him loads of weapons. So now it seems as though they might be used against us. Ironic isn't it?"

"Do you think there will be a war, Alan?"

"Yes, I do. The main issue now is whether it will be a war with or without the approval of the United Nations."

The phone rang, Thelma answered it. It was Joyce reminding her that they were coming up to see her and Sam.

Sam was now not a well person. On the last couple of occasions they had been with him, they had both noticed how slow he was to reply to anything that they had asked or told him about. This all went through Alan's head as he sat there while Thelma prepared their evening meal. But when she finally put it on the table, his thoughts about his favourite Yorkshireman disappeared when he saw what was on his plate. While he had been in Portugal he had eaten very well. Fish dishes were a delicacy in the restaurant he had eaten in almost every evening. Arenque, Besugo, Caras de Bacalhau and Mero Legitimo were the names of things he had eaten and could remember the names of and there were other things too.

But nothing quite compared to what was before him now: pork and rhubarb pie, mashed potatoes and mushy peas all covered in Thelma's lump gravy with mint and almost certain to be followed by her unique Tonyrefail tart. What would Pedro, Estevao and Gaspar, his eating companions from Porto for his last few meals think of this Lancashire-Welsh delicacy? And all washed down with a very tasty bottle of Portuguese wine that he had brought home with him.

Not surprisingly, he was late into work the next day and as he walked into his office he saw a note which read.

Boss.
Don't put your passport away. You'll need it today. We are going to Ferrybridge.
Your obedient servant
Tariq.

8. The sermon on Mount Pleasant

"Cliff is very quiet today. Do you think we should disturb him?"

It was a miserable day outside; so after eating their lunch, they would normally have played cards. But today it looked as though Cliff was far too engrossed in what he was reading to join them.

"Cliff. Are you playing cards with us today?"

Silence.

"Cliff. What are you reading? It must be good. Either that or you are fast asleep."

Silence.

"Cliff. Don't you know that this is Deaf Awareness Week?"

Cliff put the magazine on his table, took his feet off his chair and said: "No. I haven't heard about it."

"Do you know, I've never read anything as funny as this for ages."

"What is it?

"It's an article written by Tom Evans who used to work in the Paint Shop about three years ago. I told you about him last week after Allan Rooney interviewed him on *Try Time*."

Tom Evans was the secretary of the Ashurst Rugby League Supporters Association and the editor of its fanzine *The Forward Pass.*

"He was in Victoria Hospital recently for an operation on his heart and he's written about what happened to him when he was in there. It's hilarious and you don't have to like rugby to have a laugh. Do you want me to read it out to you all?"

"Do we have a choice?"

"No, but you'll still like it, you mark my words."

"You always say that."

"That's because it's always true."

And with that Cliff began to read it out loud:

A big thank you from the secretary

I would like to take this opportunity to thank all those members who took the trouble to send me get well cards while I have been away. I can honestly say that I thoroughly enjoyed reading both of them. I would also like to thank the staff at Victoria Hospital for their loving care and attention, although I must confess that on my first day I was very upset to be woken by a surgeon and a nurse arguing over which hammer to use to break my sternum and then having to wait while a decision was made at a call centre in Rochdale.

My meeting with God

During my operation I died and went to Heaven. There I met the Guardian of the Pearly Gates, a man from Miles Platting who used to follow Broughton Rangers. He told me that God is a woman and a rugby league fan too. When she heard that a Saint had arrived, she came down and chatted with me for well over an hour.

The Book of Revelations

She told me that she spends much of her time unravelling some of the great mysteries of life on Earth. At present she is working with a team of accountants trying to find where all the new money for rugby league went to in 1995. Her findings will be published in a new Book of Revelations.

She went on to tell me that her favourite teams were St Helens, Wigan St Patricks, Wigan St Jude's and Leeds Parish Church. All the others she has equal love for, although she did confess that Salford Red Devils, Hell FC and Hell Kingston Rovers often test her patience to the limit.

Familiar faces appear

On my second day there, I met Eddie Waring. He now works on a religious programme called *The Sermon on the Mount Pleasant* aided by a student called William Webb Ellis. He was amazed to learn just how many sites have been named after him on Earth. I also spent time with Nicky Tolstoy. He is writing a new version of his classic novel *War and Peace* but has changed the title to *Peace and Peace*.

Later I read that Inverness Travellers, Redruth Rovers, St Asaph Ecclesiasticals and Featherstone Academicals have reached the semi-final of the Pebbles Alcohol Free Challenge Cup.

The games will be played at St Austell and St Neots, both grounds being fine examples of all standing, non-smoking centres of humility and love thy neighbour. Each employs a catering manager who can feed crowds of over 10,000 people with five Peaceburton loaves and two sad fishes.

A match made in Heaven

On Sunday I watched Oxford University Philosophy Department beat the Blackbrook College of Media Studies in the Harry Stottle Memorial Trophy. Regrettably *We will rock of ages you* was being blasted at the crowd, most of whom would clearly have preferred to be quietly discussing the meaning of life. Before kick-off, both teams were introduced to the referee, her husband and 13 children after which they all held hands and recited Malcolm Lord's Prayer.

There have been a few changes to the game as I once knew it. It's one point for a drop-goal, two points for a penalty, three points for a try and six points for a conversion. One other change is the size of the crowds. Last month, York Cathedral captained by the former Saints' player Bishop Chavasse, beat Wakefield Holy Trinity in the Yorkshire Bible Study Challenge Cup Final at Church Fenton, watched by a well behaved crowd of over 37,000 Jehovah's Witnesses.

A bit of a come down followed

The next day I spoke again with God in her humble six storey cottage at a place called Bishop Burton. She said that she had decided to send me back to Earth to carry on with my good work with the ARLSA. On re-entering Ward 15 I was told that a young nurse had been sleeping in my bed, but had just left. I almost swore. I did when I looked under the bed and saw 10 ASDA carrier bags along with a note from our beloved chairman saying 'Please deliver these magazines to newsagents in Nook End, Astley and Gillarsfield' but with the note 'Don't carry too many at once, Tom. Make extra journeys.'

Was it all a dream?

I don't think my visit to Heaven was a dream, because I can definitely remember a gent from Billinge asking me to sign his petition objecting to the *Church Weekly News* running a series on rugby union's best 100 tries. His intellectually fine-tuned, morally uplifting and ecumenically based argument was that if printed it would encourage the telling of lies since there had never been that many tries scored.

Later this little ray of sunshine told me that a group of Sunday school teachers from Monk Fryston were urging clubs to adopt nicknames that promote a gentler image of the game. Only those with their heads in the clouds could come up with such names as these:

Barrow Day Trippers
Bradford Calves
Halifax Sox of many colours
Huddersfield People of many sizes
Hunslet Budgies
Leeds Butterflies
London Little Seaside Donkeys
Rochdale Hairnets
Salford Village Pinks
Swinton Lambs
Workington Rural Village

Heartily Yours

Tom Evans MBE
(Master of Blooming Everything)

"You have to admit it's funny. It's nearly as good as *The Final Hooter* used to be and that was good."

"A mate of mine used to work with Tom when he was on nights at Hilton's. Some of the books he used to read were out of this world."

"What were they about, Tariq?"

"Space travel" laughed Shaun.

"Talking about space travel, what does everybody think about us having our Christmas party in The Moon this year?"

The Moon over Water was the name of a pub that had just opened on Bridge Street.

"What's wrong with the Wigan Arms? We've been going there for years and they always put on an excellent Christmas spread for us."

"And what might that be, Alan?" asked Jennifer as this would be her first Christmas meal with them.

"Meat and potato pie, chips and beans swimming in Gillarsfield Gravy."

"You are going to have to change with the times, Greeno. I bet your Thelma wouldn't be happy with a meat and potato pie on Christmas Day, would she?"

"Probably not. She'd rather have a baby's yed."

"Whatever is a baby's yed"?

It was Jennifer again, still learning the names of things common to those who had been brought up no more than 10 miles from the steps of Ashurst Town Hall.

"A baby's yed, is a steak pudding because the top of it looks like the head of a baby."

"Well its mint imperial what it's called. It's what it tastes like that is the most important thing for me."

"So where are we going?"

"Why don't we elect an Office Christmas Party Committee? Three people would be enough. Give them three days to do it. That would mean a day each. We don't want them making a meal out of it."

"All they have got to decide is where, when, how much and whether or not to invite Benny."

"Who's Benny?" asked Jennifer.

"Benny was once the transport manager. He always managed to get himself invited to any do that had been organised. Even after he had left, he still kept turning up and once he had started drinking, he would take over. You couldn't stop him, but then he was so funny.

"I remember one year the Pensions Department had a do. To make sure Benny didn't find out about it, the manager was the only one who knew where the venue was and he was going to make it known to the others less than an hour before finishing time on the chosen day. That afternoon he nipped out to make sure everything was all right in this secret place. He had a couple of drinks while he was waiting for the landlord to turn up. Driving back to work he got stopped by a cop car, was breathalysed and finished up in Newton Street nick and was not able to tell anybody where it was being held."

Halfway through the afternoon in walked Horace, the idiot from Wages, to collect the timesheets. Horace always had a negative attitude to anything that was happening around him. Before long, he began complaining to Cliff about a woman from Haydock who worked in Ashurst Town Hall. She wanted to be paid the same rate as a man who was doing exactly the same work as she was.

Not seeing Jennifer in the corner of the office, Horace made the comment in his opinion a woman's place was in the kitchen.

Jennifer walked back to her desk and said quite loudly to him: "Do you know what I think Horace? Women who want equality with men are all guilty of low expectation."

Not quite sure what she meant, Horace quickly collected all his bits of paper and left.

"Nice one Jennifer. You certainly put him in his place."

"He's all right in his place. The trouble is it hasn't been dug yet." said Alan

Things were quiet for the rest of the day and the following morning too was totally void of anything interesting said, learned or done. At lunch time they were joined as usual by Pete Mulholland Today he had Dave Culshaw, an OCD fitter with him. As Pete's wife worked in the Town Hall, Alan asked him about the dispute about equal pay that was brewing there among the staff. According to Pete, it was something fuelled by the extremely high salary paid to the chief executive and the bad attitude that he showed to everybody who worked under him.

"It's the same all over the place. There's an article in today's paper about it. It's a damning indictment of this government. I won't read the whole thing out to you all. I'll leave that for Cliff to do. It's his job, but I'll just read two sentences that say it all."

And then just like Cliff often did, Jennifer read out the headlines of an article written by the *Guardian's* economics editor: "Britain is on course to end two terms of a Labour Government with a greater degree of inequality than it had after 18 years of the Conservatives. Not something for a social democratic party to be proud of."

Then Dave said: "My next door neighbour is a fireman in Widnes. He reckons that he would have to work for over five years to get what the average chief executive of a multinational gets with his wages and bonuses in a month."

"I thought the whole purpose of a Labour government was to redistribute the wealth of the country. Not make it worse."

"If you believe that Howard, you'll also believe that the moon is made of green cheese."

"Well I might have believed that once, but after five years of Tony Blair I don't believe it any longer."

Then it was Jennifer again with one of her cutting comments about the political situation: "Some people say that Labour and Tory are both the same. They aren't quite the same but they are very similar. They have their differences, but they also have so much in common. In opposition, they always used to promise so much, but as soon as they were elected, they always forget all what they had promised. Didn't Gordon Brown say that he would stick with the Conservative's spending cuts just after Labour had been elected in 97?"

"That's a bit radical Jennifer."

"She's right; I can remember Peter Mandelson saying some time ago that he didn't mind people getting filthy rich. It was when he was on some political freebie in America and probably getting paid for it while still getting paid as an MP over here."

"What he actually said, Alan was that he was intensely relaxed about people getting filthy rich as long as they pay their taxes. He said it to a group of industrialists in California in 1998."

"Thank you Jennifer. We always know where to go when we want the facts."

"New Labour is an organisation that has completely forgotten everything that the Labour Party was originally set up for. It's another pro-business party. It embraces the free market and the power of the City, without question. It has little to offer the majority of the population in terms of improving the nature of society in their interests. It has no serious intention of spreading the wealth of the country a lot more fairly. In fact, the gap between the rich and the rest of us is getting wider as that article in the *Guardian* shows. If it really wanted to reduce that gap, it could start by doing something about all the tax evasion and tax avoidance schemes that big business is allowed to get away with quite legally."

"You can complain as much as you like about how things are until the cows come home, but the way things are stitched up by the people who rule this country, you'll never change anything."

"Dave, I'll give you one good reason why you are wrong. I remember people saying that we'd never stop Beeching closing Ashurst Railway Station back in 1962. Well we did stop him."

"It's closed now."

"I know that Dave, but it kept running another 20 years and it was only subsidence from the Southport Edge pit that finally saw it off."

"Maybe."

"Is it right that Alan stopped Lord Beeching in his railway tracks? I am impressed."

"He didn't do it on his own, Jennifer. There were loads of people helping him" said Pete. "I can remember my dad taking a petition round UGB and getting over 100 signatures. When he got home that night I remember how proud my mum was of him."

Later in the day, Jennifer walked into Alan's office to ask him if he would like to write an article for a magazine she was involved with.

"You see boss, I am in something that I don't suppose you will have heard of. It's a small group called The Anti-Gap League. We want to draw attention to the great gap that is growing between the top one per cent of the population and the rest of the country. We've only been going for three months and there are only half a dozen of us in it so far. We've talked a lot about what Labour is doing and not doing and now we have decided it's time for us to do something practical and so we are going to start producing a regular magazine."

"Well Jennifer that sounds very interesting. You can put my name down for one when it comes out. I'll read it, tell you what I think of it and then I can give it to Thelma for her birthday present. Have you got any major scoops to start off with?"

"For the first issue, we think we've unearthed a corruption scandal involving an MP, three Lords and a Private Finance Initiative scheme that has just been agreed. It's my sister Mary who's done all the work on it with a friend who has a job quite high up in the Civil Service, which is why it all has to be kept very hush hush, so please don't mention this to anybody. If what she thinks is true, things could get rather nasty for her, if we are not 100 per cent accurate. Another thing we are looking into as well is the issue of MPs' expenses. You wouldn't believe what some of them are claiming for."

"I think I should introduce you to our old tea girl, Hazel Hutton. It sounds as though you two might both have a great deal in common."

"Is she the one who's going to resign from the Labour Party if Blair takes us into an illegal war in Iraq?"

"Yes. So how does your group see this threat of war in Iraq?"

"George Bush wants revenge for the attack on the World Trade Centre. He also wants to strengthen America's position in the Middle East and get American control of the Iraqi oil fields. He wants regime change in Iraq and he is using a big lie as a smoke screen."

"And what is that big lie, in your opinion?"

"The link between Saddam Hussein and Al Qaeda. The fact is that there isn't one. There is more of a link between Saudi Arabia and Al Qaeda and they are firm allies of America. If the West does invade

Iraq, that will be a great encouragement for more people in the Middle East to be attracted to terrorist groups like Al Qaeda."

"So what do you think about Tony Blair and New Labour? I take it you don't like him or them."

"It's not important whether I like him as a person or not. I don't like his politics. He's not a socialist, never has been and never will be. As far as Iraq is concerned, I think that you will soon find out that he is prepared to agree to an American-led invasion. That has been quite clear ever since he went to see Bush on his ranch in Texas in April.

"Now he is trying to con us with some vaguely defined third road. Well that road will keep this country tied to America's rulers, it's leading to war in the Middle East and it's doing nothing to reduce the growing gap between the richest people in this country and the vast majority of us who live and work here."

"Very good, Jennifer. I am impressed. You will be pleased to know that I agree with all of what you have just said and I think that my friend Hazel will as well."

"Now about this article that you want me to write for your magazine. How many words do you want, do you want any photographs, how much are you going to pay me for it and can I have the cheque sent to my secret tax haven in Zurich?"

9. Christmas Day 2002

This year it didn't look like the traditional Greenall Christmas Day family gathering would take place. Rebecca was expecting her second child and she and Neil were spending the day at Neil's parents' house at Great Sankey which is not too far from Warrington Hospital. Robert was going to Amsterdam with three of his mates for a 'week of Christmas joy and love thy neighbour' and particularly so if that neighbour was a young lady who might invite any of them into her flat to have a look at some of the paintings on her walls.

Alan's advice to him had been quite simple: "Make sure that the only thing that you catch while you are over there is the plane back to Manchester."

But when Alan returned home after the last day at work, he was greeted with the news that they were not going to be on their own after all. That morning, Thelma had met a friend in Astley Co-op. Maureen lived with her son Karl, her husband having walked out on them a year ago. Since then life had been a real struggle. On reaching 18, her older son Kevin had joined the Army and now she had the added worry that he might get sent to Iraq if war did break out.

Karl was 15 and had never shown much interest in lessons all the time he had been at Ashurst St Mary's school until very recently. Maureen was sure that his great change of attitude was linked to the arrival of a new teacher. Was this her big chance to get him to get some qualifications before he left?

Then Preston Lane Printers had closed down, throwing her out of work and to cap it all, their cooker had packed up, just days before Christmas. Hearing of her situation, Thelma immediately invited her and Karl to have Christmas dinner with them. Maureen accepted the offer straightaway and then asked Thelma if she thought Alan might like to help Karl with a project from school that he had to do over the holidays. It was something right up Alan's street, she was sure.

When Thelma told Alan what she had done, he was hardly surprised. It was typical of her attitude towards other people and particularly to those who needed help, just like she had once needed some a long time ago. He was also intrigued about the project that Maureen wanted him to help Karl with, and on Christmas Day too.

Bang on 12.30pm their visitors arrived, both somewhat shabbily dressed and looking a little nervous.

"Hecky flumps Karl, you've grown a lot since I last saw you. It looks like you'll be making a fine prop forward."

This immediately set the lad at ease for his great interest in life was playing rugby. They ate the meal with Maureen and Thelma doing most of the talking and after everything had been cleared away and washed up, Alan asked Karl what his school project was all about. It was to write an essay about the history of Ashurst.

"Well Karl, two things that the people of Ashurst have always had a great interest in are work and sport. Yes."

The lad nodded.

"So if you want me to help you, this is what I suggest we do. I know a lot about the history of the town's industries and I know a lot about all the sport that has been played and watched here. So I'll just talk about what I know; then I'll put it onto my computer and e-mail it to you. Have you got a computer in your house?"

Unfortunately they didn't. His Mum's budget didn't run to such luxuries and even if they did, it might not be working soon because she hadn't paid the electric bill and they might be cut off if she didn't pay it soon.

"Well, I can print it off and bring a copy round. Are you still living in Winstanley Street?"

He was, and so Alan began to talk in some detail about all the factories in the town that he knew about, but it wasn't long before Maureen stopped him and said: "Sorry about my interrupting you Alan, but how do you know about all these places?"

"For a start I know a lot from some of my relatives. My uncle Billy worked at Hilton's as a sheeter all his life. My uncle Jack was an apprentice at Jarratt's, moved to Davis Pumps and then went to UGB in St Helens and my auntie Hilda and auntie Beryl were at Dawson's Chocolate Works before they got married."

Then jokingly he went on: "By that I mean they got married to their boyfriends. There was not any of that other funny business in them days, or so I am led to believe."

As he continued to talk, their two visitors were amazed at what he knew. Although Maureen had lived all her life in Ashurst, she knew next to nothing about its history.

"What I have told you so far Karl is mainly about the engineering

61

companies that were once here. Do you know what the other main local industry was?"

He said that he didn't, but soon realised that he did know.

"Coal mining."

"Ashurst is on what used to be the South Lancashire coalfield. I'm afraid Thatcher and all her cronies closed it all down after the miners' strike in the 1980s. You'll know a bit about that, won't you?"

He did.

"The biggest pit in the town was Southport Edge. It used to be just off Wigan Lane, near where the garden centre is now. When I was your age, there was the Duncan, Old Monty, Bank Top, Gillarsfield, Beswick and the Prince of Wales. Not far away were Bold, Sutton Manor and Clock Face in St Helens; just down past Winwick Church was Parkside and on the other side of the East Lancs Road were Bickershaw, Parsonage and Astley Green in Leigh.

Then he digressed slightly and told Karl an interesting statistic that he had obviously read in one of his history books.

"In 1880 the Mines Inspector calculated there were over 500 coal pits in Lancashire. There were even some in Rochdale, Bury and Burnley, but now they are all gone. Well maybe not Astley Green though. That's a museum now. I keep saying I'll go and have a look at it when I get time. Anyway let's carry on with Ashurst.

"There used to be a power station in George Street but that was shut down in 1948. I know that because our next door neighbour Mr Astbury worked there nearly all his life. There was also a cotton mill up Nook End, but that closed in the 1930s and all their production went to Butts Mill in Leigh. My auntie Mary worked there for a bit after she first left school. They said she could transfer with them if she wanted to, but it was too far to travel to Leigh every day."

"Travel by train, bus and tram; that's another interesting thing to know about. The town once had two railway stations. One was called Gillarsfield Junction. It was for a line from Warrington to Golborne, but it was closed just before the war. The main station was Ashurst Central. One way the track led to Leigh and the other way it joined the Manchester to Liverpool line about a mile east of where Bold Colliery used to be and then it ran down to St Helens Junction. That was closed in 1986.

"Another interesting place was the railway sheds at Hemsley. I used to go there a lot when I first started train spotting. They closed that around 1954 and all the trains were then shedded at Sutton Oak in St Helens until that was closed sometime in the 1970s."

The lad listened in amazement at all Alan knew about the history of the town. It was almost certainly a lot more than anybody else in his school did.

"Then there were all the aeroplanes in the town."

The lad looked up in amazement.

"Aeroplanes. What in Ashurst?"

Alan laughed.

"No up in the sky. After the war, there was an American airbase at Burtonwood. The planes used to fly all the way from America to keep it supplied and as they approached the base, the pilot had to ask the Air Traffic Control Unit for permission to land. He used to say something like."

Then Alan spoke in a highly exaggerated American accent: "Hi Tango Bravo Two. We are just passing over Chisnall Avenue. Which runway have you got ready for us?"

Karl couldn't believe what he had just heard, but he still continued to listen keenly.

"Two other things that I can remember about the whole area were the slag heaps and the flashes. Do you know what they are?"

He did.

"There was Mount Everest, Mount Geronimo and the Santi. Not far away were the Three Sisters at Bryn and there was another big one was at Haydock. Wars used to be fought on there sometimes."

"Wars? Who between?"

"Yickers and Earlestowners!"

"What's a Yicker?"

"Somebody who comes from Haydock."

Then he returned to what he knew about Wilkinson's and started to tell Karl about the products that were once manufactured there, and about some of the characters that he knew, but before he went on much longer Thelma interrupted him.

"Alan, that's enough. I think that you are tiring him out now."

"Thanks for all that Alan" said Maureen.

"If you don't mind typing all that out, it will really help him. I've never seen him so interested in anything from school before. Mind

63

you they've got a new teacher. He's really good."

"What's his name, Karl?"

"It's Mr Fenton. I like him. Well we all do, but he talks a bit funny."

"I think he comes from somewhere up Burnley or Blackburn way" laughed his mother.

"But then I suppose that he thinks we all talk funny in Ashurst."

"Well Karl, I'm glad if you've enjoyed listening to all that. You'll have to come again and I'll think of some other things to tell you. Maybe I'll show you our family tree as well. That is really interesting."

The lad replied in a way that indicated that he was developing a very dry and typical Lancashire sense of humour.

"Where is your family tree? Is it in your back garden?"

Later in the week Karl returned. He had a few more questions and an interesting suggestion. If he was going to write about the history of Ashurst, surely he should include writing about the people who worked in its various factories and pits. Could he also include how they spent their spare time, how did they entertain themselves, what sports did they play or watch? Obviously he had thought it up himself; excellent, he was turning into a right little brain box.

Alan started off by telling him the names of all the cinemas in the town just after the war had finished. Then there were the dance halls, just the Co-op Hall and three church halls in Ashurst. In the 1950s young people would often go further afield on Saturday night to Wigan, Leigh, Warrington and the Co-op Hall in St Helens.

After that he mentioned the different sports that people had followed. Not surprisingly the main sport in the area was the rugby. There were five teams that you could support if you lived in Ashurst; Leigh, St Helens, Warrington, Widnes or Wigan. For those who preferred soccer there were Everton and Liverpool to the west and Bolton Wanderers at Burnden Park to the north. There were also all the non-league football teams as well: eight local sides, all of whom used to play in the Lancashire Combination.

Another popular past time had been Crown Green Bowls, more for playing than watching though. At one time there had been over 50 teams in the Ashurst Thursday Night League There were 10 teams in each division with the best teams being usually North Ashurst Labour Club, Victoria Park, Hemsley Manor Park, Mathers Social Club, Gillarsfield Conservative Club and The Black Bull.

"Well Karl, do you think you have got enough material now?"

"Yes, deffo. This is going to be great."

"Well I've just got one more thing that you might want to put in."

"Okay."

"It's about the long term effect that mining has had on the town. There are loads of coal seams running underground all over the place and every now and again, the earth moves and whatever has been built above them might be in danger of collapsing. That's what happened at Wilkinson's about 10 years ago."

At this point Karl looked up at the clock for probably the third time and then asked if it would be all right now if he could leave. Alan's little lecture had lasted nearly an hour.

"Have you got a young lady to meet?"

Sheepishly he nodded and then he asked if Alan would have a look at what he was going to write before he had to hand it in.

And so the birth of Alan's second grandchild Sarah in Warrington Hospital to his daughter Rebecca and Karl's article about Ashurst's industrial past were two of the things that Alan would remember well about Christmas Day 2002. At the time the two events did not seem very important or significant. But many years later, both Karl and Sarah were to play a significant part in the life of the region and some might even say the whole country. One became a journalist on the *Warrington Guardian* and the other became a leading figure in what was to go down in the political history of the land as the Great British Bus Pass Revolution of 2025.

10. The Welsh girl from Wrexham

"So what did you do over the weekend, Alan? Anything interesting or did you just stay in bed and keep out of Thelma's way?"

It was the first time the two of them had had a chance to have a lunch time chinwag for quite a long time. Cliff's first few days in the New Year had been spent at West Burton Power Station. He returned home not feeling at all well; his doctor had declared him unfit for work and instructed him to stay at home. Food poisoning was the cause and it kept him off for another week. On the day he had returned to work Alan had gone to the Rolls Royce factory in Coventry. He didn't particularly want to make the trip, bearing in mind how bad the weather was. By the time he was back home it was Friday evening and so they were not together until the following Monday morning.

"Well, actually Cliff, I had the most stimulating, educational and enjoyable of weekends."

"Does that mean you stayed in bed, kept out of trouble and managed to read the *Sun* all the way through from the front page to the back page?"

"Cliff, as you are well aware, like you I never read the *Sun*, not unless eating some dodgy food with Richard Burton has affected what passes for a brain in your head."

"So what did you do then?"

"Robert brought his girlfriend round. It was the first chance we've had to talk to her and she is a most interesting character."

"What's her name?"

"Megan."

"Is she Welsh?"

"No, she's from Outer Mongolia. Megan is a very common name out there."

"Is she Welsh?"

"Yes."

"So where does she come from?"

"Wales, you might be surprised to know."

"Wales as in Wales or Wales as in New South Wales?"

"Wrexham, which is in Old North Wales."

"Where did he meet her? I suppose it was in Wales."

"No. He first met her when they were both at Coventry University. He bumped into her in Chester a few days after he came back from his trip to Amsterdam. They went out for a drink, got on very well, he met her again, one thing led to another and not long after she moved in with him."

"So what's interesting, unique or special about this one?"

It was a fair question for Cliff to ask. Alan often told him about the various girls that Robert had been out with before. Many of them had unusual backgrounds, strange occupations or were from out-of-the-way places. Aimee, for example had been a member of the England Women's cricket team, Claire worked in the Civil Service in London, Carol had grown up in the Orkneys and now worked as a journalist for the *Manchester Evening News* and Anne was an actress who often appeared in *Coronation Street.*

"Well, her background is a bit more ordinary than most of his other flames were. She's really nice, dead easy to get on with and particularly good with the way she uses language."

"Can she speak English then?"

Conversations like this with Cliff were always enjoyable to listen to. Alan often compared them to playing table tennis. He would say something, Cliff would retort with some clever play on the words Alan had used, Alan would do the same in his reply, twisting or misusing the words Cliff had used and each would go on in this way to and fro.

"So what did you talk about, other than how good the current Saints team are, how you used to go to Abergele for your holidays when you were a kid and how you've got some fiddle going that means you keep having to visit a cotton mill in Portugal?"

Ignoring what Cliff had said, Alan went on: "She was a bit quiet at first, but when Thelma had told her about how she had been brought up in a children's home in Cardiff, she soon opened up. She told us all about her family, growing up in Wrexham, and what most of her relatives did for a living. She even told us a bit about what life was like there in the 1870s."

"Bloody hell, Alan. How old is this woman?"

"Cliff, you don't have to be 200 years old to talk about what Ashurst was like in 1800, do you?"

"No, but it might help."

"Recently Robert has started showing interest in our family tree. I told him just before Christmas that one of our ancestors originally came from North Wales. That was something my auntie Doris told me about although she didn't know exactly where. All that she knew was that he was married to one of my uncle Jack's relatives, had an unusual surname and two of his children had died young.

"After they had been going out for a while, Robert discovered that one of Megan's interests was researching her family tree. He told her about our Welsh connection and when he mentioned the name of Barrelman, she told him that she thought that there was someone with the same surname in her family. She checked and discovered a Henry Barrelman listed in the 1861 census as a cabinet maker living in Wrexham. But when she looked on the 1871 census he wasn't there. She looked in the Ashurst census for 1871 and found a Henry Barrelman living in Nook End. She then went to the 1881 census and found him again, now living there with Alice Barrelman. That must have been his wife and they had one boy and two girls living with them as well. On the 1891 census she found him, his wife and one boy living nearby in Canal Street. So the two girls must have died.

"Now what is interesting for me is that this boy would have been about the same age as my grandparents. Canal Street is only four streets away from where my granddad's family had moved to from Fingerpost in 1899. So there is a very good chance that their paths could have crossed. Maybe they both went to the same school. Don't you think that is fascinating?"

"Well, it is if you like that sort of thing."

"Well I do."

"I know you do. So what else did you find out about her?"

"Unlike most of Robert's previous girlfriends, this one is quite left wing. She is like Jennifer, a bit of a wordsmith as well, you might even say."

"So did you tell her how about how you stopped Lord Beeching closing Ashurst Station with that petition and how you were on the DATA office committee and were once the union branch secretary?"

"It cropped up in conversation. It was after she told me that before he died, her dad had been a full-time trade union official in South Wales."

"Where does she work?"

"British Gas in Chester."

"She's not a gas board fitter, is she?"

"No, but she is certainly fit. She's a bit of a marathon runner."

"Which bit of her?"

"Her legs, I would imagine."

Alan paused for a moment before going on to say that really there appeared to be only one thing wrong with her.

"Don't tell me. She's got three kids, smokes a pipe, can't even boil an egg and doesn't know her fish knife from her meat knife?"

"No. That's four things anyway."

"So what is it?"

"It's worse than that. She actually likes watching rugby union."

"So I suppose you gave her your usual lecture about what happened at The George Hotel in 1895 and how that teacher at Ashurst Comprehensive tried to stop all the lads in your Robert's class from playing rugby league."

"And failed, don't forget. No, I could hardly get a word in edgeways. Thelma told her."

"So how much does Thelma know?"

"Quite a lot actually. She has always been a big reader, always got something on the go. Recently she read my copies of two of those books that I sent to Italy for that American guy Elmer, *Rugby's Great Split* by Tony Collins and *At The George* by Geoffrey Moorhouse. There's loads of stuff in them about the history of our game. That is how she was able to tell Megan so much."

"Well done, Thelma."

"You can say that again."

"Well done, Thelma."

"It was clear that Megan knew little about the history of the two games and how the rugby union authorities had for nearly 100 years tried at every turn to stop people playing rugby league. She was amazed when Thelma told her that although many rugby union players did go North for the money, many others couldn't afford to take any drop in income or found out that they would have to pay income tax if they did switch to playing rugby league."

"She was really surprised when Thelma told her how the Vichy Government in Occupied France had co-operated with the Nazis and passed a law to ban rugby league. She didn't even know that until union went professional in 1995, if a union man played just one game of rugby league for a professional club, even without being paid, he was not allowed to play rugby union ever again. She just didn't believe it."

"I bet a lot of people in Wales didn't know that either."

"She told Megan about how an England international from Bristol in the 1930s had considered switching codes. He came up North to meet officials of the Warrington club. He had talks with them, but decided that he didn't fancy moving so far away from his family and went back home. Somehow the Rugby Union found out and banned him from playing and all he had done was talk. I don't even think he got his expenses. In fact the first time he actually saw a live game of rugby league was on his television about 20 years later."

Just at that point, Colin came back into the office. He had been out shopping as he often did on Thursday lunchtimes. In WH Smith he had met an old work mate who told him that the rumours about Hilton's Assembly closing were no longer rumours. All those still employed there would be out of work by the end of the month.

Alan knew a lot about Hilton's, because his uncle Billy had first started work there in 1932 and continued to do so all through the war. He had never been called up because he had failed every medical examination he had ever taken. Auntie Kitty would often say to him when he was going out: "Be careful Billy, try and hold on to something. There's a little breeze blowing out there."

He would often reply by telling her not to worry because he was a big city boy. Big he wasn't, only five foot two tall and weighed little more than eight stone. A city boy he was though, but only because he had been brought up in Seddon Street in Windle City in St Helens, within sight of the City Road ground where St Helens Recs had played until just before the outbreak of the war.

Both of them had been dead for over 40 years, but Alan still had fond memories of them. All the time he had been at Hilton's, uncle Billy had worked shifts. Three days on six-two, one day off, three days on two-ten, one day off, three days on ten-six, two days off.

Auntie Kitty had also been on shift work at Dawson's Chocolate Works: five days on earlys, then five days on lates, but no working on a Saturday or a Sunday. But for the last few years of her life she didn't work at all. The work she had done on munitions during the war had given her a skin ailment that no doctor seemed able to cure.

What didn't help either was the fact that she smoked incessantly, though it never appeared to affect her. Uncle Billy smoked only now and again, maybe as many in a week as his wife smoked in a day. Sometimes, if she had run out and it was too late to nip to the shop, she would ask him if she could borrow some of his, hilarious really, particularly when she would return the next day with a couple of packets and carefully put what she owed him on the left hand side of the mantelpiece.

When Alan arrived home later that day, Thelma greeted him with the same news that Colin had told him earlier, Hilton's were closing. She had heard it while shopping in the Co-op. Later that evening his neighbour Phil called round to discuss the issue with Alan and get some advice. Hilton's had changed greatly since uncle Billy had worked there. The number employed had dropped from nearly 1,000 to around 100 and the new bosses had few, if any, good management skills. All they ever did was obey the latest set of instructions sent from the owners in America, after their weekly board meeting.

Phil was the shop foreman, but he still held his union card and did not want to see the factory close. He knew that if the women on the shop floor could be persuaded to stand together there was a chance of keeping the place open. The problem there was that only a few of them were in the union and the one person who might have been their leader had the nickname 'Red Martha'. She liked to think of herself as a bit of a fighter. She had even been known to have a row with her own shadow. If she could only be persuaded to use her brain before opening her mouth, she would be their best bet.

Phil knew, from what Alan had told him, about how Wilkinson's' draughtsmen had often got the better of the owner Basil Wilkinson.

It was one of Alan's ideas that Phil took into to work the following day. The man in overall charge of the company was the American, Claude. He was only in the Ashurst factory on Thursdays and Fridays. For the rest of the week he would be found at the company's other factory near Dublin. His assistant was Roger, a local man who Phil knew could be very helpful if handled correctly. There were a few things about Roger that could be used, the first one being that he did not want to lose his job, secondly, he did not like Americans and hated the way Claude made him do all his dirty work, and thirdly his wife was a friend of Phil's sister Sandra.

So with this in mind Phil walked into Roger's office the next day and told him of his plan to attempt to save their jobs. Then he went onto the shop floor, convinced Martha to go and ask Roger if their union could have a formal meeting with him about this growing threat of closure. The best time for her to do this was in the middle of the afternoon. Martha agreed and so accompanied by one of her members, she did just that as Roger was making his afternoon brew.

His response to what Martha had asked was exactly what Phil had told him to say: "If you lot want to be in a union, you can all piss off home now."

In saying what he had, Roger had not said anything about the girls not coming back the next day and he had said it with less than an hour to go before finishing time. All this made it easy for Martha to get the whole production line to walk out and have a meeting in the car park. However, none of those who worked upstairs in the Box Shop came out. Their self-appointed leader was a loud-mouthed bruiser called Sheila. She was very anti-union and told all her girls to go into the canteen to have a meeting and agree not to walk out. Maybe she had some understanding with Claude, there had been rumours about the pair of them before, so she felt happy with her action in his absence; or so she thought. All her girls trooped into the canteen to listen to her tell them what a stupid rabble the women downstairs were by walking out.

It was around this time that Roger received his daily phone call from Claude. On hearing that nobody was working, he went ballistic. He told Roger to tell everybody who was not at their normal place of work that they were sacked. So the ridiculous situation arose in which all those who did not want to join a trade union were going to lose their jobs for being at a meeting to agree to not to join a trade union.

To protect his own position, using more advice from Phil, Roger told Claude that he would not be in work the following morning because he had a hospital appointment and suggested that Phil should be left in charge. Did Claude want to speak to him? He did and so Phil found himself negotiating a simple solution to the situation he had so cleverly engineered.

Phil immediately told Claude exactly what he had to do to get everybody back in work. It was for him agree to formal talks with the local full-time official of the women's union and implement whatever was agreed for all who were members.

Claude had no alternative. The penalty for the late delivery of an order now on the shop floor would have ruined his budget and may even have cost him his job. Phil added that he wanted it in writing so would Claude send an e-mail. As soon as that was received Phil could guarantee everything would be back to normal.

Within the hour the e-mail arrived with all the wording that Phil had requested to the effect that in the event of a redundancy occurring in the next 12 months, all those who were union members would receive their full redundancy money.

The following day everybody turned up for work as normal. The first thing Phil did was to talk to Martha and tell her of their success and to get someone from the union's office in Liverpool to bring 100 application forms straightaway. Then he went upstairs and told Sheila to inform all those who had gone to her meeting what Claude had agreed to. Most of them decided that it was now in their best interests to join the union, even Sheila, though very grudgingly. As things finally turned out, it didn't actually stop the company closing the place down nine months later, but all the redundancy money owing was paid out in full, something which Phil later discovered that the company had never intended to do if they could have got away with it.

11. "There's a dead body up here!"

The houses in Silkstone Street had all been built in the 1870s. Number 22 was where Alan's grandmother had been born in 1892 and lived almost all her life. Her parents had raised seven children with granny being the fourth to arrive. The others were Katherine, Doris, Eric, Arthur, Hilda and Kitty, all now together again buried in Windle Steps Cemetery. When granny was 12 years old, her mother had died and so she had had to finish going to school and become the little mother to the rest of the family. Six years later she had started walking out with Ned Holding who lived nearby in Alfred Street. A couple of years later they were married and begun to raise a family. Grandad had died in 1982 and soon after granny had gone to live in the Greenfield Old People's Home in Dob Lane. As she left, Alan, Thelma, Rebecca and Robert left their first home in Beswick Street and moved in.

As a small boy at Lane Head Junior and Infants school, Alan had been a frequent visitor to the house and was known by many of the neighbours. Two in particular had always had a soft spot for him: Mrs Pilkington who lived next door at 24 and Mrs Higham who lived at 67. Mrs Pilkington had lived on her own as long as Alan had known her. That was because her husband had drowned during the evacuation from Dunkirk in 1940. At number 20 lived Mr and Mrs Whittle. During the war, he had served on the battleship HMS Rodney and the minesweeper HMS Cromarty. During those times she had been employed on munitions work along with his auntie Kitty.

The way that the houses in the street had all been built meant that granny had much closer contact with Mrs Pilkington than she ever had with Mrs Whittle. Stood on the pavement at the front, a passer-by could see that the distance between the front doors of 20 and 22 was little more than a yard. However, the distance between the front doors of 22 and 24 was much greater. That was because between them were the two sitting rooms and living rooms of each house. Much longer though was the wall between 20 and 22. That separated their entrance hall, the stairs up to the bedrooms, their living room, kitchen, pantry, wash house and outside toilet.

At the back of each house was a six foot high wall which divided their yards and what passed for a small garden. At the bottom of each yard was a wooden gate which provided their access to the back entry. As a result it was easy for granny to stand outside her kitchen door and call out over the wall to Mrs Pilkington. If Mrs Pilkington heard her and granny wanted to have a little chat, she would get a pair of steps out of the wash house, climb up and look down on Mrs Pilkington who would bring out a chair from her kitchen. It clearly wasn't the way granny could communicate with Mrs Whittle though. To do that she would have to go out of her front door, down four steps onto the pavement climb up four steps in Mrs Whittle's front garden and knock on her front door.

Mr and Mrs Whittle were long gone and number 20 was now owned by Alan's neighbour Phil. Until 1997, he had lived there with his wife Cynthia, but she had died quite early in life and Phil had carried on living there on his own. Then purely by accident he had bumped into a widow on the M62. Well, actually it had been through an accident that he had bumped into a widow on the M62. He had been driving past Burtonwood Service Station heading towards Manchester. So had she. As a result of a collision a few cars in front of them, she had braked quickly. He had not braked quite as quickly and driven into the back of her car. While waiting for the police to sort things out and get the cars moving again, they had chatted. Her car had to be towed away and so Phil had driven Janice back to her home on the outskirts of Oldham, which as luck would have it was not far from his destination that day which was Miles Platting in north Manchester. He stayed for a drink of tea and chatted for a while. One thing led to another and four weeks ago she had stayed with Phil for the weekend. They did not see Phil over the following weekend, but seven days later they saw the pair of them again looking quite happy and now spending more and more time together.

Silkstone Street was a nice friendly street mainly because most of its residents had lived there a long time and knew each other, particularly at the top end. There had been a lot more changes down at the bottom end though, partly due to the presence of a betting shop, a Chinese takeaway and a mini market. This all made worse a problem that now existed across all the built up areas in many towns, trying to find a place to park the car. There just wasn't enough room. The second problem at the bottom end was the Rathbone family. The parents had little control over their children. Fortunately two of them were currently guests of Her Majesty and the third one was finding it difficult to even stand on the pavement, due to a broken leg he had suffered in a brawl in the Colliers' Arms a month earlier.

Another troublesome thing was the existence of a large family of mice who inhabited the lofts at the top end of the street. Every now and then they would be heard running round. As soon as that happened Thelma would go on 'mice alert'. She would climb up a ladder that they kept in the back bedroom, to reach the loft hatch and pull herself up onto the boards, go round and set the traps. While she was up there she would have a look round and make sure everything was all right. And that was what happened one Friday afternoon just around the time that Alan was due to arrive home from work.

As Alan came into the house, he saw Thelma's front door key on the table so he knew she was in. As he took his coat off he heard a terrible scream. He rushed up the stairs and saw the steps on the landing and the loft hatch open. Then he heard Thelma shout: "Alan, come up here quick. There's a dead body here."

Now, Thelma had developed a wicked sense of humour and a few times she had fooled him or their children with some little trick or other, but that was not how it sounded today. Whatever could have happened? What had she seen? He was soon to find out.

When she had climbed up into the loft, in her hand she held some cheese and a torch she had recently bought. Twice as bright as the one they had previously used, it showed up much more than the old one had ever done. She had crawled round on her hands and knees and shone it on a chest of drawers that had been there for years. Propped up against the wall behind it was a picture frame that she now wanted to look at. So she had pushed the chest of the drawers to one side. In doing that, she had exposed not only the picture frame but also a hole in the wall, which separated their loft from next door's loft. It was just about large enough for her to crawl through.

She was soon in the loft above what had once been Mrs Pilkington's front bedroom. Three things caught her eye, an old suitcase, a pile of newspapers and a canvas sheet about three yards long and a yard wide. It was just as Alan was opening the front door that she had crawled over to look at what lay underneath it. Supporting her body on her left hand, she carefully used her right hand, still holding the torch, to lift the sheet. As she did so her left hand slipped, her right hand moved the cover and as she fell her face touched the bones of a human skeleton. It was hardly surprisingly that her touching it with her cheek had made her scream out loud.

She was clearly in a state of shock so they went downstairs into the living room and Alan poured her a large glass of Pernod. A second one went down as quick as the first one did. Then she washed her hands and face twice.

Alan phoned the police to report what they had found. The person who answered the phone was surprised, and said that they would send someone round as soon as they could.

Soon after he put the phone down, it rang. It was not the police, but Rebecca, their daughter. Who better than her for Thelma to talk to for the next five or 55 minutes, long enough no doubt for Alan to return to the scene of the crime and have a look for himself. The skeleton might have been there as a result of a crime, but it must surely have been a crime committed many years ago. He could hardly imagine Mrs Pilkington having done it. She didn't even like killing flies.

He crawled through the space and saw the suitcase, the pile of newspapers and the human bones. He removed the suitcase and the newspapers and put them on the floor in their back bedroom. He knew that the authorities would have to come and remove what was left of the deceased. A forensic scientist might have to visit first though to look at the body, give his opinion on when the person had died and whether it was of natural causes or something worse. And if there was anything suspicious, that might involve a police investigation. His first glance at the contents of the suitcase and the age of the newspapers though interested him greatly and why should anybody else take them away and then probably class them as of little interest and lock them away or even throw them away?

He decided the thing to do next was close the loft door, go downstairs and offer to go to ASDA to buy another bottle of Pernod for his wife. But when he walked into the living room Thelma was still on the phone to Rebecca and they were talking about holidays so clearly she had overcome her frightening experience.

Within 10 minutes a police car was round and not long after all traces of the skeleton had been removed. The officers said that someone would be round to see them in the morning.

After tea, they had a quick look at the contents of the suitcase. In a strange way her contact with the skeleton had made her want to know more about who the man or woman was. They agreed that when they informed the authorities, they should say nothing about the suitcase or the papers.

That evening they went more carefully through the contents of the suitcase. Whoever had packed it had obviously had an interest in local history. There were newspaper accounts of incidents at a number of collieries in the area. There was also an account of the railway trials at Rainhill in October 1829 when the Liverpool MP Lord Huskisson became the first person in the land to be killed in a railway accident.

They also saw material written about the sinking of the first shafts in the 1870s at what later became Bold Colliery and, on a totally different note, memories by someone who had been a schoolboy at St Theresa's school in Nook End, providing graphic examples about how cruel some of the nuns who taught there had been towards the children. There were also copies of *The Ashurst Globe* and *The Ashurst Weekly News*, which had both ceased publication in the 1930s and a photograph of Ashurst Town Hall, taken three days before it burned down in 1893.

A policewoman came round the following morning and took statements from them both. She said they had found details of the deceased in a pocket of the clothes under the skeleton. His name was Thomas Gee, his address was a house in Earlestown and the only bit of information on him was a wage slip from the Vulcan Foundry in Newton-le-Willows. After she had left they looked through the suitcase again, but there was no mention of him. Maybe he had been a lodger or a friend or maybe an enemy of someone who had once lived next door. It would have been well before Mr and Mrs Pilkington had lived there though and something that might never be known.

There was one other twist to the whole affair. Thelma brought the picture frame down into the living room on Saturday afternoon and decided she liked the frame, but not the painting. So she had opened the back of the frame to remove it. She discovered that there were two paintings there and between them another old copy of the *Ashurst Globe*. Its main story was very interesting to Alan. It was an account of the official opening of Ashurst Railway Station by Lord Billinge who then owned much of the land in the area.

Two pages were given over to 'Births, Marriages and Deaths'. Most of this was devoted to the latter. In each case the name of the deceased and their occupation was provided. This was followed by the names of all those who had attended the funeral, the name of the church and who had officiated. Among the names he noticed were those of Pickavance and Bacon. Was there any chance that they might be long dead members of Alan's own family? There was nothing there that went back as far as 1791 though, which was a pity since this was as far back as he had been able to trace any known relatives.

He looked at the section devoted to Marriages and read of the wedding of two people who had the same surname, John Tabern and Catherine Tabern. The name was quite common round Ashurst and there were even Taberns in his family tree. Maybe this was something he should let Megan look into. He didn't have the time to do it himself because there were a whole host of other things he had promised Thelma he would do in the house. He had also offered to help Robert fit a shower in his flat in Latchford and then just last week Rebecca had asked him if he would help Neil build a shed at the back of their house. There just were not enough days in the week to do it all. Still he would think of something, he always did. Or maybe they might all be prepared to wait until he had retired and then he would have plenty of spare time.

One thing that he had put off doing for some time though was going up to see his old mate Charlie. He hadn't been up to Donkey Common for ages. He decided that it was something he would do first unless, of course, something else got in the way like being asked by Mr Johnson to return to the Portuguese town of Familicao, or to Gyor in Western Hungary or maybe now to Murcia in Southern Spain, although sadly never to Accrington again.

12. Billinge rules

It was Friday lunchtime. Alan, Cliff, Colin, Shaun, Tariq and Howard were sat in their usual spot in the Eagle and Child, but the atmosphere in there was not good. The bitter was off, in the sense that it was still being sold, but was far from pleasant on their taste buds, the place was cold because the heating was also off, the music from the juke box was too loud and two young men sat near them who had probably been in there since the place had opened a couple of hours earlier were arguing loudly.

"It's not like the old days" said Alan

"Once upon a time we could have had enough lads in here to pick two rugby teams and a referee."

"At least we've got enough for two table tennis teams."

"Cliff, when did you last play table tennis?"

"Last Sunday. We had Louise with us for the afternoon."

"Did you beat her?"

"No. She won, as usual."

"Is she good at it?"

"Very good."

"How old is she now?"

"Five."

"Five. I wouldn't have thought she could have got it over the net."

"We don't have a net. We have to play to Billinge rules. That is how she says we have to do it. That's how they do it at home."

At this point they were joined by Ray Eccleston. He lived nearby in Mersey Street and this was his local. He was the younger son of Charlie Eccleston and things took a turn for the better when Alan asked him how his dad was.

"He's not bad. It's his birthday next week. He's either 83 or 84. He's not quite sure."

"I'll have to come and see him."

"He'll be really pleased to see you now that he's got his new glasses. Tell you what, we are organising a little birthday party for him. Why don't you fetch some beer and that'll save the wife having to go and get them?"

"How many are coming, Ray?

"We are not quite sure yet. He's invited all the current Saints team as you would expect him to, all the members of the 1966 Wembley team who are still alive or not living Down Under, a few regulars from the Vine, and some lads from the Bowling Club. I think he's going to invite Billy Boston as well and tell him to bring some Wiganers with him, just to make sure things don't get too intellectual."

"Typical Charlie. Yes. I'll fetch all the beer in. I'll get a loan for it."

"You don't need to come alone. Fetch your Thelma. We'll need somebody to do the washing up as well."

"What day will it be?"

"A week on Thursday."

"Oh I am sorry, I can't get that day off. I've got a big job on at Eggborough."

"That won't be a problem, Alan. Just give us the money and I'll do it for you. I don't mind. I've plenty time on my hands."

Alan put his hand in his pocket, took out three pound coins and apologised that they wouldn't go far.

"You can pay for it electrically if you prefer to. Just give us your library card. That will probably fit in the machine. You can have it back tomorrow. It will be easy that way."

As he was speaking, one of Ray's neighbours walked into the pub.

"Hey Ray. I've just seen your Maud at the top of Newton Street. She's waiting for you to come home with the dinner."

With one large gulp Ray emptied his glass, muttered something along the lines that his memory wasn't like it used to be and left.

As he walked out Frank shouted out: "Do you know what she's got in her right hand eh? A bloody big rolling pin."

Minutes later the door swung open again and in walked another familiar face from the past. It was Dave Hollinghurst, who had once worked in the Mechanical Section of Wilkinson's Drawing Office and was now working in Warrington.

Alan stood up, shook his hand and introduced him to the others.

"So where are all the rest of them?"

"Dave, this is all the rest of them. There's not many more of us left now, what with all the redundancies and Computer Aided Design. It's not like it used to be when you were with us."

"Well I'm sorry to tell you that there is one less of us now. That's why I've called in; to tell you that Jack Large died on Tuesday."

"He was killed in a bloody stupid accident, right outside his house, run over by a cyclist. It was bloody tragic."

"Why? What happened?"

"He was getting shut of some furniture, giving it to his grandson Tom. He opened his front door and the two of them started to carry a table out of the house. He stepped onto the pavement walking backwards, not bothering to look if anybody was coming down the street. Unfortunately there was, a young kid riding his bike on the pavement. He hit Jack full on. They rushed him to Whiston Hospital, but he was dead before he even got there. Tragic, absolutely tragic."

"How's his wife, it was Beryl wasn't it."

"Hell of a state. She's been ill for quite a long time. I wouldn't be surprised if this doesn't see her off. Poor soul."

Dave then reported on some other old timers who he had seen recently: "Les Fishwick and Dave Langton both work on the tills at ASDA, Harold Campbell does mornings in Cancer Research and I've seen Bernard Harrison driving the 329 bus to Warrington a few times."

But the oddest bit of news was still to come: "There is something else that I have heard, but I don't think that you'll believe it. You remember Ken Brightside, that ginger haired foreman in the Copper Refinery."

"I do. He was the main man in Ashurst Labour Party, social secretary of Hemsley Labour Club and a local councillor as well."

"I bet that you don't know where he is going tomorrow?"

"Probably to some Labour Party meeting of lost souls somewhere I expect."

"No. He's going to London on that demonstration against the threat of war in Iraq."

"You're joking. He's not been on a demonstration since that Vietnam one in Grosvenor Square in 1968 when he couldn't find his coach to come back home in."

"It's true. His niece is in an anti-war group of students at Ashurst Tech. There's a bus load of them going down and she's convinced him to go with them. He keeps telling everybody that he doesn't agree with Tony Blair and all his New Labour policies; and now he has even gone as far to say that if Blair agrees to an invasion of Iraq, he will resign from the Labour Party."

"I'll believe that when I see him do it."

"If you stand outside the Town Hall tomorrow morning at seven o'clock, you'll see him getting on the bus.

"So, will it be a case of Blair in, Brightside out? Well that's unbelievable. He must have been a member for over 50 years."

At this point, Benny appeared with a pint in one hand and a pie in the other. Theoretically he had retired, but from time-to-time, the management asked him to return to help out.

As he sat down, Colin turned to him and said: "Eh Benny are you still a member of the Young Socialists?"

Before he could reply, Alan chipped in: "How could he be, he's neither young nor sociable."

"I once bought Harold Wilson a pint in Whiston Labour Club. Does that count?"

He took another swig from his glass and went on: "Do you know what Marx wrote about politics?"

It seemed a bit of an unusual question for Benny to ask unless, of course, it might just be a lead in to a joke.

"Politics is the art of looking for trouble, finding it, misdiagnosing it and then misapplying the wrong remedies."

"Where did Karl Marx write that?"

"Who said anything about Karl Marx? It was Groucho Marx. He also once said that military intelligence was a contradiction in terms. He must have been thinking about Saddam Hussein's weapons of moss destruction. Anyway have you noticed that whoever you vote for, the government always wins?"

'Madam, before I get through with you, you will have a clear case for divorce and so will my wife' and 'marriage is a wonderful institution but who wants to live in an institution'. That's another one of Groucho's sayings."

"It sounded like two to me."

"Ted Ray was even better for misusing English and punning. I backed a horse at Aintree yesterday at ten to one and it came in at quarter past four."

This was just how Benny liked to enjoy life, a drink in his hand and an audience to listen to him talk and once he got started he was so difficult to stop. Before he could say much more, Alan was interrupted by one of his staff, Joan, asking if it would be all right if she left early as she had to visit the doctor's. Then Colin spoke about another famous person well versed in the use of the English language, the American actress Mae West. He had recently read her biography and so proceeded to repeat some things that the book described things she was supposed to have said like: "I'll try anything once, twice if I like it and three times to make sure. Another one was "I generally avoid temptation, unless I can't resist it" and "when choosing between two evils I always choose the one I haven't tried before."

Not to be outdone though Benny had to get the last word in when he commented that Mae West was the sort of woman who had climbed the ladder of success wrong by wrong.

Back in his office 20 minutes later, Alan was going through some papers that had landed on his desk while they had been in the pub when the phone went again. It was Benny.

"I just thought I would let you know that my mate Arthur is moving to Seoul next month. He reckons it will be a good Korea move."

"No I didn't know that. Thanks for telling me."

"And did you know that the Keystone Kops were often accused of the excessive use of farce?"

"Benny, I somehow suspect that the Transport Department hasn't got much work on this afternoon. So however have you conned them into letting you come back in here?"

"Just this afternoon we are a bit slack. Not like where my sister Joan works. It's in a sweater factory in Salford. They are a good set of folk there. They could be described as a very clothes knit community."

"I take it that you wouldn't find it too difficult or inconvenient to have 40 winks this afternoon"

"Alan, it would not be the least bit difficult. For me sleeping is easy. I can do it with my eyes shut."

"Benny, toodeloo. Johnson's coming. A'll sithee tomorrer."

"Tha waint, if ah see thee fost."

Alan put the phone down just as the boss walked into the office, turned round and walked out again.

"Who was on the phone?" asked Cliff, now keen to get started on a drawing which might lead to him having to visit the Bottling Plant in Spain that Dave Morris had recently returned from.

"Benny, with a few more classics from his new found political mentor Groucho Marx."

Ten minutes later, Mr Johnson reappeared. He walked into Alan's office, shut the door, sat down and said: "I have some important news that is for you and you alone."

He began to shuffle the papers in the folder he had brought with him, put some on Alan's desk, some by his left foot, some by his right foot, took a pen out of his pocket, bent down again to pick up the top sheet from the right hand pile, coughed loudly, keeled over and literally dropped dead.

A nurse from what was left of the Works Surgery was called and within half an hour the body of Mr Johnson was on its way to the morgue at the back of the Town Hall.

By this time Alan had gathered together the papers that Mr Johnson had brought with him and put them away in a drawer. Those marked 'Confidential' he would read as soon as he got the chance to do so. They might just be dealing with the issue of redundancy. Maybe this was what Mr Johnson had wanted to talk to him about.

Mr Johnson's death was the first thing he told Thelma about when he arrived home. She had left Wilkinson's a long time before he had arrived on the scene and so his departure meant little to her, although she did know how little time Alan had for him. Then he told her about Ken Brightside's threat to leave the Labour Party.

She had known Ken very well and recalled once going to a public meeting in North Ashurst Labour Club just before the General Election in 1964 when Harold Wilson had been the main speaker and Charlie Eccleston, who claimed to know him well, had introduced the future Prime Minister to Ken, Alan and her.

It was a pity she hadn't seen Charlie for ages, even though it was less than five miles up to his house in Thatto Heath. Maybe they should find time soon to go up and take him some of her delightful Welsh scones. He was now living on his own because his wife had died a year ago. Despite now approaching 83 or 84 he still managed to play bowls, watch the Saints when they were at home and do his own shopping. Luckily for him his sister lived in Rainhill and his eldest son Paul in Stafford Road and they both kept an eye on him.

She remembered how he always described himself as a simple working class lad from St Helens. Simple he wasn't, working class he certainly was and proud of it. It was a pleasure to have known him and to have known him well. If only there were a lot more people in

85

the world like him, then the world would be a much better place for us all to live in.

Then she told Alan that Megan's mother had been taken ill and Megan and Robert had gone over to visit her in hospital in Wrexham. Unfortunate really, because they had already arranged for the four of them to go to the Reebok Stadium in Bolton that night to watch the World Club Championship between the Saints and Sydney City Roosters. Everyone had been looking forward to a close and entertaining game and it would have been a good introduction for her to the game of rugby league. However, as things turned out it wasn't to be. At half-time the visitors were winning fairly easily, 18–0. At the end of the game, that score had been extended to 38–0 so perhaps it had been a good thing that Megan had not gone. Hopefully, Bradford Bulls at home the following week might be better introduction for her.

It was. Her mother had quickly got better and so Megan was able to relax and watch the Saints fully in control right from the start of that game and won an entertaining match 46–22.

And on the way back to Ashurst, she had said something that the other three people in the car were very pleased to hear her say: "Now I know why everybody round here calls rugby league the greatest game of all."

13. Martindale's chip shop

Jennifer had now been in the Drawing Office for over six months and had certainly made a big impression. She had raised the quality of discussion on whatever was being talked about and was always able to provide facts and figures to prove anything that she spoke about. This was due to the way that her parents had brought her up and because she had a very good memory for things that she had seen on the television or heard on the radio. Also she could able to recall what people had said that morning, earlier in the week, or even weeks or months ago. She was also a big reader, this being 'helped' by the fact that she never needed more than five hours of sleep at night.

At home she had a very regular routine. She always watched the *10 o'clock News* and *Newsnight* with her parents and then discussed with them what they had just seen. Within minutes of getting into bed, she would be fast asleep, but by around five o'clock she would be fully awake and ready to start reading her latest book. As a result she would read more in a week than most people manage to read in a year. In this way she accumulated an enormous amount of knowledge that was useful, interesting and often quite controversial.

She had also been strongly influenced by her experiences growing up as a child in the North East, during the miners' strike in 1984 and 1985. Two uncles and a cousin had been heavily involved in that bitter dispute; all three were active members of the NUM. Her parents had been active too by helping organise a miners' support group in their village. One particular event then had made a big impression on Jennifer. It was while her auntie had been looking after her one afternoon, she then a playful six year old in her small terraced house at a place called Peterlee. Suddenly the front door had burst open and into the room had burst three burly policemen looking for some young man they wanted 'to talk to'. For them, he was just another Geordie Bolshy bastard. For her though, it was her cousin David.

Another influence on her had been her great grandfather, although she had never met him. He had taken part in the Jarrow March in October 1936. Sadly though, soon after returning home he had passed away, but what older members of her family had said about him made her appreciate what a wonderful and well respected person he had been.

In the office every Monday morning, she would invariably get asked what earth-shattering events had she been associated with over the week-end and today it was Alan who asked her the question:

"So Jennifer, did you go on that 'Not in My Name' demonstration in London on Saturday?"

"Afraid not, Alan. I would like to have gone, but my mum came out of hospital on Thursday after her operation and my sister Mary came up from London to see her."

"I'm sorry to hear that. How is she now? Is she getting better?"

"Yes. It was serious what she had, but she's recovering now."

"So what did you do then over the weekend?"

"Well, one thing that we did do was to play a really funny trick on our next door neighbour. My mum just sat there and watched us doing it. It was really good seeing her laughing her head off."

"You've never told us much about your sister. What is she like? A stunning beauty, highly intelligent, multilingual, ideologically sound, musically qualified, politically correct and a pain in the backside for most of the time, just like you."

"You certainly have a way with words Alan, but all the wrong ones mis-coupled together."

"Go on then. Tell us. I'm sure it's going to be worth listening to. They usually are from you on a Monday morning. That block cable diagram you are working on for Fiddlers Ferry can wait for a bit. I don't think they will need to generate much electricity until after they have had their tea break this morning. It is quite a warm day."

"When I got home on Friday, there was a skip outside the front of the house. It was for our next door neighbour Henry to get rid of a load of rubbish from his garden. Mary was there, first time she has been up to see us for ages. Anyway, the pair of us decided to play a trick on him. He's a lovely old guy, but I don't think he knew that I had a twin sister.

"The following morning, when we saw him out at the back, I went out there and Mary went into the front garden and started trimming the hedge. He talked to me for a few minutes, then picked up a bag of rubbish and went into the house with it. Two or three minutes later he threw it into the skip at the front, saw our Mary there, but thinking it was me he just smiled at her. He went into the back garden and saw me again. I could tell he was a bit surprised, but he said nothing.

He picked up another bag of rubbish and did the same journey through the house and again saw Mary at the front. By this time I had gone into the house and waited until I could see that he had put the second bag in the skip. When he came back into the house, I told her to come inside our house so that the next time he appeared there would be no one there. We sort of carried on doing this for about half an hour. At the end of it, he was going mental."

"And was that the highlight of your weekend or did you take Mary to watch Warrington for another good laugh?"

"No. The moment I mentioned watching any rugby she said 'no way'. She had a good reason for saying that too. Her friend's husband plays union for Wasps and they had been to watch him a couple of times. The first time they went, Mary thought it must have been the worst bit of entertainment she had ever seen and could not get any worse. That was why she agreed to go again and it was worse. Me trying to tell her that rugby league was different from rugby union would just not wash with her."

"So, as well as worrying an old man, what else did you do?"

"We spent Saturday night listening to her tell us about some of the places she had visited when she was working in America. Then on Sunday evening my boyfriend came round and we had a long discussion about what is going to happen to the world banking system. Mary reckons it is going to crash, within the next three years or so."

"So what does she base that on? Where does she get all her information from?"

"A lot is from her personal experience working in the financial world ever since she left university and also from friends who also know more about what's going on. She's worked for two major banks in London and one in New York and since she been back in England she's been with a firm of insurance brokers based in Canary Walk. On top of that one of her former boyfriends was a hedge fund manager and her current flame is a trader at Barclays. So that's how she knows so much about international finance. It's all very fascinating stuff, but quite disturbing and frightening too."

"And all you can say for yourself is that you work with a bunch of semi-literate Lancashire draughtsmen. I bet she feels really sorry for you."

"Not at all Cliff; I met a few of her friends before she went to America. If they were typical of the rest of them, all I can say is that I am much better off with you lot, despite all your ill-mannered ways."

"Jennifer, we can't carry on talking like this for much longer or else it will interfere with our preparation for the tea break. Why don't you tell us more about this economic situation over lunch? You see I desperately need some sound financial advice. On Friday night I went for a pint in the Gas and Electric Club and won £10 in a raffle. I want to know what to do with it. Which bank will it be safest to put it in or should I just hide it somewhere in the house where I know Thelma will never find it?"

"To be honest Alan, I don't think any bank is totally 100 per cent safe today because what are increasingly dominating the world money markets are neo-liberal economic dogma, risky investment programmes aimed primarily at raising bankers' bonuses and absolute greed at the very highest level. Not something to inspire confidence for anyone."

As she uttered the last word, the door opened and into the room strode their new boss, Mr Musgrove. He had taken over after Mr Johnson's sudden death. Bizarrely, although he was in charge of the Drawing Office, he wasn't a technical man. His qualification to do the job was an honours degree in business studies.

He immediately fired a load of questions at Alan, but few were of a technical nature. How much work did the office have on at the moment? When would those jobs be finished? How well acquainted with electrical safety standards in various Eastern European countries was Alan? Were everybody's passports up to date and could the office be given a thorough tidy up? He wanted answers now because soon one of the top brass from Amsterdam would be arriving.

Alan provided satisfactory answers to everything he had been asked. He suspected that the most important question related to the general untidiness of the office. In Alan's opinion, that was irrelevant. In Mr Musgrove's opinion though, that would probably be the most important thing because whoever turned up would see that as important. Well, he would do if he had been come from the same mould that Mr Musgrove had come from.

Within minutes of leaving, Mr Musgrove phoned him with news about their visitor: "Alan, I have just been informed that our Dutch friend will be here sometime later today. He will be staying at the Hemsley Hilton and his name is Mr van Dijk."

Was this the same Hugo van Dijk who had visited them soon after Koen Koevermanns had taken over Wilkinson's in 1993? If it was then it was good news. Hugo was a great character, a wizard with the computer and a man with many tales to tell about himself going back to his childhood days in the Dutch town of Looperkallersalle. There would be no need to try and impress him.

Soon after, he had a call from Dawn in reception, telling him that she had a visitor there for him. It was the man himself.

"Alan, my friend, I am very pleased to make again your acquaintance. How are you? How is your lovely Thelma and how are your beloved Saints? Have they won since I was last here in your beautiful city of Ashurst?"

Same old Hugo, despite him being 10 years older and dressed as though he was going to Buckingham Palace to meet the Queen. They went straight upstairs and into Alan's office.

Hugo sat down and explained that there were three reasons for his visit. Firstly the company had subcontracted a lot of work to a firm in Rotterdam, but a fire there had caused damage to their machine shop and reduced their drawing office to ashes.

Most of the drawings had been backed up on the company's hard drive system, but not all of them. What was needed urgently was a team of draughtsmen to sort everything out. They would have to check all the power and control schematics, the panel assembly drawings, block cable diagrams, and if some had not yet been done, to draw them.

All this could not be done in the office in Amsterdam. They just did not have enough people to do it and their machine shop was full of more urgent jobs. Hugo knew how co-operative Wilkinson's had been in the past, hence the reason for his visit. As he spoke he looked out of the window and saw Jennifer sat in front of her computer.

"Who's that?"

"Jennifer, our expert on tariff metering."

"The other thing is we might need someone to come over to Amsterdam every other week. Perhaps she could come."

"I know what you are thinking, Hugo. Don't bother, but I'll still introduce you to her and everybody else in a few minutes. There have

91

been quite a few changes since you were last with us."

"Before you do that Alan, the first thing I have to do is to talk to your Mr Musgrove. What is he like?"

Alan pulled his face.

"No words are necessary. I understand. I'll tell him I don't want him involved in anything. It's going to be me and you, Alan. Now two important questions: When will you be taking me to watch the Saints again and when can we eat in Martindale's chip shop and have one of those, what do you call them, baby's yud, I think?"

"Baby's yed, chips, peas, gravy and a barm cake, twice."

"How about baby's yed, chips, peas, gravy and a barm cake for three, me, you and Jennifer perhaps."

And with that, he asked Alan to show him where Mr Musgrove worked and where he would tell him that Hugo wanted the work done as he wanted it all done and no interference from anybody else.

Twenty minutes later Hugo was back. Mr Musgrove had been told the score and would not be bothering them. He then rubbed his hands and asked Alan what they should do next as they had time to kill before they could be the first to enter Martindale's chip shop.

"Bad news, Hugo. Martindale's are shut this week. They are putting a new fryer in. But I know a very good place in Leigh were we can eat."

"Where is Leigh?"

Alan explained that it was his intention to go to Bolton that morning to a bakery to discuss the details of an order they had just placed. Hugo could come with him. Alan expected to be finished by noon so they could come back into Leigh and dine in a place on Railway Road and still be back in Ashurst by mid-afternoon.

"Before we set off, I'll just introduce you to the rest of my team, then we'll have a drink and after that, Bolton, here we come."

And so within an hour of walking into the Drawing Office, Hugo was sat in the works van on the A579 heading towards Bolton. It was a good opportunity for the two of them to hear what each had been doing since their paths had last crossed, now nearly 10 years ago.

Hugo began first in some detail what had happened to him since he had last been in Ashurst: "When I first met you Alan, I had only been with Koevermanns for about six months. But shortly after, they offered me a permanent position. Then they began sending me on jobs all over the world. I bet I have been in more electricity substations than any other engineer in Holland and I am not kidding.

"About a year later I had a bust up with one of the directors and walked out. A few days later I discovered that my younger brother had been murdered. He had been in trouble with some low life and everybody knew who had done it, but the guy thought he was untouchable. I never told anybody what happened next, but by the end of the week, his body was found in the canal and soon after I flew out to start a new life in Australia, or so I thought."

The story he then told seemed a little difficult to follow. It seemed quite unusual, but it did mean that the journey time just flew by. Even the time spent in Bolton passed quickly and soon Alan was parking the van in Dorning Street in Leigh. They had a meal in the restaurant on Railway Road, paid a visit to that well respected centre of learning, the local history section of Leigh Library and then had a quick look at Hilton Park. As they walked back to the van and with a dead pan face, Hugo asked: "Alan, is there a brothel in Leigh?"

Alan burst out laughing.

"Hugo, you have more chance of sharing a table with the Pope in Martindale's next Monday than you have of finding a brothel open this afternoon in Leigh."

"Why is that?"

"Because today is early closing day."

Alan returned Hugo to the Hemsley Hilton and arranged to pick him up in the morning. Tomorrow evening he was invited to Silkstone Street for a meal and to meet Thelma again. Then on the Friday evening they would take him to watch the Saints play at Knowsley Road. During the rest of the week Alan laughingly told Hugo all the members of his team had been instructed by Mr Musgrove to be on their best behaviour and impress him with whatever they said or did.

"There is no need for that, Alan. Not one little bit. My mind was made up before I even got on the plane at Schipol. Your little gang has just won the raffle. First prize is the design of an oil fired power station in a place called Cordoba in Argentina. It will be very similar to that power station design you did for us at Alkmaar.

"Can I also suggest that you go and get yourself a 'teach yourself Spanish' manual. I think will be very useful because I think that at least one or two of you might well have to go out there quite soon."

14. Canteen talk

The following morning Hugo explained in detail what he wanted doing first and that whenever a job was nearing completion, a Dutch engineer would carry out a quality control check. Once any equipment had left the factory any problems on site would be his responsibility, but it would be useful if whoever had done any design work would to be prepared to go out on site if necessary.

By the end of the day though, Hugo's plans for the week had been changed, following a long telephone all in Dutch. It had been his intention to stay for a week, but some urgent family business suddenly required him to return to Looperkallersalle. But he fully intended to be back in Ashurst in good enough time to watch the Saints next game, this time at Widnes on 8 March.

By lunch time on Thursday, all of the existing work going through the Drawing Office had been finished or put on hold and Alan had organised a meeting in the afternoon with Cliff, Colin and Howard to work out who was going to do what. It was another miserable day, so nobody went out at lunch time, except of course for Jennifer who always did her shopping on a Thursday. As usual, Cliff was sat reading his *Guardian* while eating his lunch. Whenever it carried an interesting or controversial story, he liked to read it out loud to all the others, whether they wanted to hear it or not. And today he had something very important to quote from the front page: "Britain's dirty secret. This is Falluja 2, identified by Colin Powell as an Iraqi chemical plant. Confidential documents show we were warned, but we helped build it. And we covered it up."

No one said a word and so he carried on: "A chemical plant which the US says is a key component in Iraq's chemical warfare arsenal was secretly built by Britain in 1985 behind the backs of the Americans, we can disclose. Documents show British ministers knew at the time that the £14 m plant, called Falluja 2, was likely to be used for mustard and nerve gas production."

"So what has that got to do with us?"

"Well, Horace, the odds are that we are going to go to war with Iraq and if we do, they will be using weapons that our government has sold them, against British soldiers."

"That's a disgrace. That's just typical of this Labour government."

"Sorry to upset you Horace, but this was done in 1985 and that was when your beloved Mrs Thatcher was in charge."

Horace had just walked into the office to query some timesheets with Alan. His prejudices and ignorance were well-known as was his argumentative attitude to anybody whose views clashed with his.

When he saw which paper Cliff had been reading from, he snorted: "How do you know it's true? Just because it's written in that commie rag doesn't mean it happened. It was probably the Russians that built it, anyway. You can't believe anything that load of idiots write."

"So what does the *Sun* say about Falluja, Horace?"

"I don't know. I don't read the *Sun* and I don't know who Falluja is either. I bet he's some lazy benefit scrounger who hasn't done a day's work in his life."

"Actually Horace, Falluja is a woman."

"I guessed as much. She should be sent back where she's come from."

"I've been told that she comes from Wigan."

"I'm not surprised I've never met anybody from there who was ever any use."

"My sister in law lives in Wigan, Horace. Do you think she is of no use and do you think that Jennifer should be sent back to Sunderland, where she comes from?"

At that point the phone rang and Horace quickly used the opportunity to get away. He never failed to demonstrate his ignorance on all matters of importance to the human race.

"I don't know how he's managed to keep his job here when you think of all the decent people who have been finished."

"I think he was lucky with illness, Cliff. When that last big redundancy was on, he was in hospital having his appendix removed."

"I don't know about having his appendix removed. I think he was in hospital having his brain removed."

Then Alan chipped in with a story from the past: "I remember once there was a sales rep in here around the time there had been a lot of gang warfare in the town. It was one of the main topics of conversation and Horace said that the way to prevent any more trouble was to build a six foot brick wall at the top end of Billinge Road near to the Folly Arms. That would stop all the troublemakers from Wigan getting into town on a Saturday night. This rep then said that he thought that was a bit extreme.

"So Horace asked him if he was new here and the bloke says that he didn't actually work here. He was the sales rep for the biggest supplier of electrical control gear in the North West. And then he ran his hand over his head and said very loudly: 'If they build a wall at Nook End, how will I manage to get here from Bolton. I suppose I'll have to drive across Fairclough's Field and go through Judy Woods. Or maybe I won't come at all and where will this firm be then?'

"Everybody burst out laughing and Horace slunk off straightaway and we didn't see him for ages after that. Bloody idiot."

"That's all very well, Alan. But what I've just read is serious stuff."

"I don't disagree with you, Cliff. I just hope that this Hans Blix guy gets more time to prove that Bush and Blair are wrong and there are no weapons of mass destruction in Iraq."

The phone rang in Alan's office. He went to answer it, waved Cliff in and asked him a couple of questions. Then he gave him the phone to speak to a fitter who was ringing about a query on a job in a carpet mill in Toulouse. By the time they had walked back into the main office, Jonty from the General Office was there eating a large meat and potato pie that he had just taken out of the microwave.

"Do you know what I miss, Alan?"

"What's that?"

"Having us dinner in the old canteen"

"'Having us dinner', don't you mean 'having my dinner'?"

Jonty repeated the statement, though slightly differently: "Having me dinner in the old canteen."

"Eh Jonty. How often did you eat in there? I thought they had closed it before you arrived on the scene."

It was Pete Mulholland, a regular visitor at lunch time.

"No, he did used to eat there during the first month he was here." said Cliff.

"That's when they closed it, when they saw how bad his table manners were."

In its heyday, Wilkinson's canteen was an amazing place. It was divided into 11 sections. Two for the preparation of the food, five where it was served plus the offices, the toilet block, showers and store room. In the evening, parts of it were used for badminton, table tennis, and space for members of the cross country, rugby and football sections to get changed. And often on a Saturday evening, all the tables and chairs were removed and it became a place of entertainment for those who liked to dance.

"I bet it wasn't as big as the canteen at the B.I."

It was John, a wages clerk who had just called in to see Tariq. His father and grandfather had both worked all their life for British Insulated Callenders Cables in the Wire Mill at Prescot.

The phone rang. It was for Alan again and so as the others continued eating, he had to deal with a problem that a fitter had just encountered at Eggborough Power Station.

It was five minutes later before he was able to put the phone down and as he did, it rang again. And so it was another 10 minutes before he was able to resume eating and talking.

"I'll tell you what I will miss if you want to know."

"What's that, Alan?"

"Having my last dinner with Accrington Sally tomorrow."

"What has she got to do with it?"

"That second phone call was from Billy Tunstall. He's just told me that he can't start dismantling our machines for at least another week. By the time I get there, she'll be gone."

"Why?"

"The pub she works in is closing down tomorrow."

At this point they were joined by Frank Walton, who had just returned from a job at a cotton mill in Portugal. No matter where he went, three things always seemed to happen. New problems were discovered on site and discussed at great length on the phone; an order, often quite large, was placed for more electrical switchgear and things happened in his hotel that just had to be told, always to the amusement of whoever was lucky enough to be in his company.

On hearing what they had been talking about, he began to tell them about the canteen he had eaten in while he had been away: "When I arrived, they put me with an electrician called Pino. We spent an hour going over the drawings I had brought and then at half 12, we went to the canteen. It was a massive place. We each picked up a tray and started to pick food from the counter. I didn't know what was what so I chose whatever he chose. By the time we got to where all his mates were sat I must have had about seven or eight plates of food on my tray plus a bottle of wine and a bottle of beer.

"He started off with a drink of wine, then onto the soup. After he had eaten half of it, he pushed it to one side and started on a plate with little fishes on it. I finished all my soup off, ate my little fishes, then something that looked like carrot, but wasn't, then another piece of fish with potatoes. He moved onto a piece of lamb with gherkins off another plate. He had also started on the bottle of beer and I was nearly full. He carries on with different vegetables off another plate. He just went on and on like this and then, you had to see this to believe it. He emptied what was left of his wine into his soup, lifted up the plate and supped it.

"Then we all got up and walked to the counter and he gave the girl on the till, two tickets and took us next door where they were serving wine and spirits. That part of Portugal is famous for brandy, so he gets us one and asked if I wanted a beer to go with it. I don't know if he ate like that every day or just because it was all free with me being with him. I never found out because the day after, he went on nights and I never saw him again."

Then he turned to Alan, looked at what he was holding in his hand and asked: "Don't you want the rest of that butty?"

The phone went again for Alan. It was from Cockenzie Power Station, a few miles outside the centre of Edinburgh.

By the time he had returned the others were talking about some of the people who used to work in the old canteen.

"My grandmother worked there during the war" said Frank. "She wasn't a waitress though; I think she just peeled the spuds."

This inspired Alan to start to tell a tale from his own life and times when he made what at first seemed a ridiculous statement: "The first time I ever ate in the old canteen was in 1945."

But before he could tell them what happened next, the phone went again, yet another problem to be sorted out with another engineer who was clearly in the right place with either the wrong drawings or not the latest issue of the right drawings.

Twenty minutes later he came out of his office, and started eating his pudding. As he looked up Mr Musgrove stormed into the room.

"Alan, how long do you lot have for your lunch. It's nearly half past one. You really must set a better example to your staff."

The reason for Mr Musgrove's visit soon became clear. The price for an order for a foundry in Dusseldorf, which he had failed to progress before he went on holiday, had to be with him by the end of the day. Normally it would have taken Alan a full day to do all the calculations. Now he was being asked to do it all in an afternoon. If he did do it before five o'clock, what would that mean? He would be expected in future to estimate on jobs of a similar size in less than four hours. Talk about creating a rod for your own back

"Well I think I can just about do it. But it will be a big rush for me"

"Good man" muttered Mr Musgrove.

"Where should I bring all the paper work to?"

"Bring it to my office. I'll be staying here until around six tonight. I've got to go to a meeting of the Rotary Club this evening. We are organising a charity event for the Walton Lane Hospice."

"You said that you wanted it ready by the end of the day. For me the end of the day is midnight. So will you still be here then or will you come back in for it?"

"No, I can't come back and I have to go up to Carlisle first thing in the morning for a meeting with Scottish Power, so you'll have to have it ready first thing Thursday morning."

And by first thing on Thursday morning Alan was ready to show the boss how the job could be done two different ways, with differences in price, number of men involved on the shop floor and on site, all of which was a little bit beyond Mr Musgrove's appreciation or comprehension.

"If I had rushed that job, I could easily have been £20,000 out on my estimate" he told Cliff later on in the day.

"If you had rushed everything through in four hours, you wouldn't have had time to work out how you could have wangled your way to going out on site either."

"I don't know whether it's good or bad that Musgrove doesn't have the slightest idea what we do here. I bet he doesn't even know what Ohm's Law is. He's just as bad as Johnson ever was."

"Do you know that just after he had started here, I think it was when you were in hospital, he was told that there was going to be a two week delay completing a machine that was due to be delivered to a steel mill in Poland. At the same time, there was an order going through the shop for four almost identical machines for a steel mill in Hungary, so Musgrove sent an instruction for one of these to be sent instead. It obviously seemed a good idea to him because the two places were only about 50 miles apart, on each side of the border. What he found hard to believe was that in Hungary the earth wire is red whereas in most other countries it is green and yellow."

"Alan, although this place is still called Wilkinson's Engineering, does it have any connections with any original members of the Wilkinson family?"

"None at all now Tariq. I think that the only one who is still alive is Cyril's widow. She wouldn't be any good for running this place though. It used to take her 10 minutes every morning to decide which side of the bed it would be best to get out of."

"How do you know that?"

"Well it's probably true. She was never very bright. She once asked me why the light inside her fridge was always on. Wasn't that a waste of electricity, she asked?"

"And did you know what the answer was or did you have to look it up somewhere?"

"You don't get an HNC without knowing why. Do you know?

15. "Will you be our auntie Thelma?"

"Has anybody seen the cards?"

It was a miserable day, definitely one to stay in the office during the lunch break and play cards. But they couldn't play cards today because no one could find them.

"I bet your Dutch friend has taken them with him back to Looperskoobydobydo" laughed Colin.

Hugo was now back in Amsterdam and so was no longer around to amuse them with tales about some of the places that he had lived in and worked at. This had included not only in his home town of Looperkallersalle, Amsterdam, Volendam and Rotterdam in Holland but also Madrid, Milan, and Malmo and others much further afield like Bangkok, Manila and Saudi Arabia. As a result, while he had been with them, there had been never been much need to resort to playing cards to pass the time away.

"I suggest that we spend some of our lunch break learning how to speak Dutch. I'm sure he'll be inviting us all over there soon."

"I thought he said we should start learning Spanish." said Colin. "I've already started. Does anybody want to hear me say good morning, good night and how much?"

"Niente senor"

"I suppose we could play I-spy."

"Go on then, since it must have been me that lost the cards. I get blamed for everything else that goes missing. I'll start. I spy with my little eye something beginning with Z."

Ten minutes later, with no one having said a word, Cliff asked if they had all given up.

They had.

"It's ZT/42/42001/R."

"You can't have that."

"I can. It's the number of that Siemens drawing on the wall."

"But I can't see that out of the back of my head and Colin can't see it because he hasn't got his glasses on and you can't see it either from where you are sitting."

"I can."

"OK then, clever dick, if you can see it, what's the name of the guy who drew it?"

101

Cliff screwed his eyes up and said: "It looks like someone called Baron von Munchen Gladback and it was drawn on 13 October 1998."

"I know what would be a lot more interesting to do." said Colin.

"We could have a competition to see who has been to the most power stations."

He knew he was sure to win because he had served a five year trade apprenticeship with the CEGB.

"I've been to Agecroft, Aberthaw, Blyth, Cocknezie, Drax, Eggborough, Elland, Ferrybridge, Fidlers Ferry, Kearsley, Rugeley, Thorpe Marsh, West Burton and Stella West."

"All right Colin, you've won. Can we talk about something a little bit more interesting?"

"You never mentioned Bold in your list."

"Strange isn't it. I lived in Sutton for a while. I could see the cooling towers from our front garden and yet I never managed to go in there, though I went past it often enough."

"I once had a trial at Hoghton Road in Sutton."

It was Pete Mulholland.

"Were you found guilty?"

Ignoring Alan's question he carried on: "When I was 18 I played football for Sutton Parish. St Helens Town organised a couple of trial games so I thought I would see what my chances were. There must have been about 40 young hopefuls there. They picked two sides of 11 and about half a dozen more and told the rest of us to go and play on the waste land at the back of the goals. Just as we started playing a bloke in a tracksuit turned up and joined in. Well, he was brilliant. He must have scored every time he got the ball. I couldn't understand why he wasn't playing on the main field. After a while we packed in and went to watch all the others. When we got back in the dressing room this mystery player had disappeared. I asked one of the club officials who he was, and why he hadn't been in the trial?"

"He can't play for us. I wish he could. He plays for England."

"It was John Connolly, who played for Burnley and lived about 20 minutes' walk away. Well he did then."

"So was that a case of one of the best players in England playing against one of the worst players in England."

"Something like that. The next game I played in was against UGB at Bobby's Lane up Eccleston near the Griffin. I broke my wrist that day, went to Whiston Hospital with it, met a young nurse there and started playing with her instead."

"You went to Whiston Hospital with your broken wrist. You could hardly have gone without it, could you?"

"Did you ever play any sports, Jennifer?"

She had just returned from town with a very heavy shopping bag.

"I reckon she must have been a weight lifter, judging by what she always brings back from town in that bag every week."

"Swimming, of course. And I used to like running when I was growing up in Sunderland. One day when I was 10, I ran away from school. And when I was in the sixth form I once helped run a raffle."

"How about throwing the discus, or maybe throwing all your wastepaper into your paper bin now and again?"

That was a sly dig from Colin at Jennifer's general untidiness.

"I am not even prepared to discuss it."

"So what are you doing this weekend, Jennifer? Are you going on any anti-war demos or will you be at Wilderspool watching Warrington on Sunday?"

"No, I'm going to a competition."

"What, a beauty queen competition?"

"Thank you Alan for that compliment, but no. It's a brass band competition in Blackpool."

"Are you a brass band man then? You never said owt."

"If she was a brass band man, Pete, she wouldn't be wearing a frock, now would she?"

"Well, she wouldn't if she was playing in Ashurst, but you know what they are like in Blackpool. There's all sorts of funny folk there."

Then Cliff chimed in again: "There's a few strange folk in Billinge and they all live next door."

"And do they all play in a brass band?"

"No, I think they all play in Boy George's Band. They certainly dress up like he does."

"I bet Jennifer likes Boy George."

"Afraid not Alan. I'd rather listen to the Brighouse and Rastick."

"Really?"

"Yes and a few others like the Beatles, The Animals, Gerry and the Pacemakers and the Blessed Six."

"That's a bit more like it" said Colin "although I've never heard of the last one. Are they some Geordie band?"

"It was the band my dad played in when he was a lot younger. He was their drummer."

"There used to be a lad here who played in a band called The Rainmen in the 1960s. Ask your dad if he had ever heard of them. They were pretty famous at one stage. Well they were round here."

It was true. The lead singer was John Rigby who came from Prescot and had worked at the B.I. until he had joined Wilkinson's Drawing Office in 1963. They were called The Rainmen because two of the band lived in Rainhill and one came from Rainford.

Just talking about Riggers, as he was known then, brought back a few good memories for Alan. At the time, the members of John's band were not good enough to give up their day jobs and go full-time. As a result they often played late night gigs and then turned up for work at eight the next morning, which partly explained why John was forever nodding off during the day. But, somehow he seemed to manage to live that way until he had decided to go contracting in Holland and little more was heard of him or his band.

Thus, it came as a big surprise the following day when Jennifer came into work with news about the Rainmen. Her dad had spent a couple of years working around the clubs in Holland with a Newcastle band when he was a lot younger. Not only had he got to know John, but on a couple of occasions had played drums with his band when their regular drummer had been 'incapacitated'. But that was a long time ago and the two had never been together again as her dad had returned home shortly after and then met a girl from Durham, now Jennifer's mother.

John was a few months younger than Alan, which meant that he was now almost 63. Where was he, Alan had often wondered. Where were all his old mates from those past times now? How many of them were still working? How many of them were still living within a 10 mile radius? How many of them were still living in Britain? How many of them were even still alive?

There was Graham Simister for a start. Alan had shared a desk with him at school and they had been good pals for the first two years. But then he hadn't appeared in the third year. Alan learned why a few years later. His parents had come into money, moved from Ashurst to live on the Wirral and had enough now to send Graham to a boarding school. There one of the first things that he had been taught to do was to get rid of his Ashurst accent.

Then he remembered some of the lads he had been friendly with when he was an apprentice, Jack Taylor for example. A very talented lad was Jack. At the age of 30 he was a senior engineer, but by the time he was 40 he had left Wilkinson's and gone to work for NASA in America on space research. Another former friend of sorts had been Ronnie Kershaw, who had decided at an early age that crime did pay. He had moved to Manchester and worked as a visitor, which meant visiting people's houses when they were not in or were fast asleep in bed. Then he moved to Sale and continued to engage in criminal activity at a more profitable level. But he soon fell out with a 'friend', got set up and knocked down and now was in long term residence in Strangeways Prison.

Helen Murdoch, the former bus conductress was another one. He had been rather lucky with her in the sense that he never went out with her. One Friday afternoon going home on the bus, he had asked her for a date and when she agreed he was over the moon for she had quite a reputation. On Saturday afternoon he had been injured playing football and finished up in Victoria Hospital. He had been due to meet her that evening outside the Gas Showrooms and when he hadn't turned up she had gone off with a lad from Portico. What neither Alan nor this unfortunate lad knew was that a week earlier Helen had had a one night stand with an old friend and was now pregnant. For Alan, his injury had been an example of how a bad thing can be turned into a good thing.

With these thoughts about the past swirling around his head, Alan drove home. As he walked into the house he heard the sound of people talking. Well that was nothing unusual, the number of people who called in to see Thelma for one reason or another was quite amazing. But then she was that sort of person, a good neighbour or a good friend, particularly if someone wanted a bit of help or just a chat to share a problem. And so it was today.

He walked into the kitchen and saw her sat at the table with two little girls. She got up straightaway and ushered him into the living room and told him that they were the granddaughters of her friend Beryl. She had been looking after them for the last few months because their mother was in hospital, but now Beryl had to go into hospital herself and had rung Thelma to ask if she could look after them for a few days.

That was no problem at all for Thelma. They could both sleep in the back bedroom, the same room that Thelma herself had first slept in on that never to be forgotten Christmas night in 1962.

"No problem is there, Alan" she had asked, knowing full well how he would reply and so things changed quite a bit in the Greenall household for a while.

Beryl was not in hospital very long, but when she came out Thelma insisted that she stayed with them until she had fully recovered. It then transpired that Beryl's daughter was not in hospital, but in prison. Her life was a mess. Her husband, who was a waste of space, had left her and if Social Services had got involved, they might have taken her two girls into care.

The four weeks that the girls stayed were really enjoyable for all concerned. It was just like the old days when Alan and Thelma had played all the usual games with Rebecca and Robert: Snap, Snakes and Ladders, Hangman, doing jigsaws, reading bedtime stories, and showing the older girl Tracey how to make a cake.

On their first Saturday Alan and Thelma took them out for the day. They went on the train to Lime Street station in Liverpool, walked down to the Pier Head, took the boat over to the Wirral and then went on a bus to New Brighton where they had a meal. What a treat that was for the girls, because neither had ever been on a boat or even seen the sea before. Even more surprisingly, they had never even travelled on a train or eaten out. But then, there had never been any spare money around in their house for treats like the ones they had just enjoyed. Their father had drained it all away in the pub and the bookies while their mother had had to struggle through each day as best she could.

Now it was going to be different because when Jasmine heard how well her two girls and her mum had been looked after by Thelma, it made her determined to turn over a new leaf. As soon as she was released from prison, with help from her mum, she was determined to start her life afresh, free from all the misery and grief that her former husband had given her. She wouldn't know then how long it would be before she saw him again, not that she ever wanted to. He would now be in Walton Jail for the next nine years for his part in a gang related vendetta that had led to the death of a lorry driver at Spike Island near Runcorn. By then the girls would be in their teens and hopefully everything in their lives would have changed permanently for the better.

It was not until the end of March that Beryl was well enough to return home with her two girls. Thelma drove them there, helped them settle in and promised to call round every week to make sure they were all OK. And just before she left the house, Thelma received a lovely reward. The youngest girl, Cheryl, asked if she and her sister Tracey could call her 'auntie Thelma' and would she like to come to her birthday party, which was the following week and on the very same day that her mother would be coming home.

As she drove back to Silkstone Street later that afternoon, Thelma thought again about the time she and Beryl had lodged together with Beryl's auntie Lil. It was during 1962 and a time when the pair of them were saving up and planning to go and work in London. If Beryl hadn't found out that she was going to have a baby, they would surely have both gone together. Getting pregnant just then had been a great misfortune for Beryl, but on the other side of the coin, it had helped things turn out well for Thelma and she knew it.

She would not have got the job at Wilkinson's, she would not have met Alan on Christmas Eve and all his family and especially his granny the next day and she would never have become the mother of Rebecca and Robert. And now she would never have become the auntie to Cheryl and Tracey, a nicer pair of little girls you could never hope to meet.

Thelma went up again at the weekend with a suggestion that seemed obvious. Why didn't Jasmine and the girls move in with Beryl? There was enough room for all four to live there, the girls could continue to go to the same school and Thelma would make sure that she behaved like a good auntie and for the next few weeks began to call round regularly to make sure everything was all right.

And as things turned out it was.

16. 10 Grasmere Avenue

"Do you know where we are going to tonight?"

"No. Give me a clue."

"Guess."

"To Thatto Heath to see Charlie?"

"No."

"To see Joyce and Sam?"

"No."

"Bed, straight after I've finished all the washing up?"

"No."

"I give in."

"Nothing new there then."

"So where is it and will I be coming back?"

"Your departure time is in 20 minutes. You'll know then."

The phone rang and as he went to answer it, Thelma suddenly felt worried. He had used the word departure, he hadn't spoken much all the time they had been eating their tea and his behaviour seemed strange this evening. Was he now going to say he had had enough of her? Was he now going to kick her out? Were all the good times living with him coming to an end? She sat there waiting for him to finish his phone call and discover her fate.

Although he didn't give the appearance of it, Alan was in a very good mood. The office pools syndicate had just learned that the pay-out for second dividend was almost £2,000. Unfortunately, that money had to be shared among nine of them, but even so it was not to be sneezed at. Also, Mr Musgrove had told Alan that he was sending him to a pharmaceutical company at Patras in Greece to discuss a potential order for electrical switchgear for a new substation.

The company was near where Alan's old school friend Winston had an apartment. He had an open invitation to stay there if he ever wanted to. Also, it was not that far from Thrakomakedhones, which was where Thelma's father had grown up. If he stayed at Winston's place, then Thelma could go with him and visit the town. It was all something which she knew absolutely nothing about. At the same time, Alan did not realise that the way he had behaved that evening, with this trip on his mind, had upset her.

Around half seven, Alan parked the car outside the butcher's on Haydock Lane and they proceeded to walk into Grasmere Avenue. They went past numbers two, four, six, eight and then stopped. They were now stood outside number 10, the house in which Thelma had once lived with her friend Beryl. At first glance it looked little different than it had done back in 1962, some 40 years ago.

"Let's have a look inside."

Grasmere Avenue was on the opposite side of town and Thelma had never had any particular wish to see the place again. Suddenly she found herself returning to her past and she didn't feel too comfortable about being there.

She held his hand tightly, fearing there might be some ghosts from her past there. He opened the gate, now clearly on its last hinges. They walked down the path and looked in the window of the front room. Then Alan did a most unexpected thing. He took a key out of his pocket and opened the front door. Thelma remained silent. This was so weird. Stupid thoughts began to circulate around her head. Was he now going to return her to where she used to live? He had hardly said a word all the time he had been in the car.

They stepped over a load of unopened envelopes and newspapers and went into the main room. It was obvious that whoever had been living there recently did not place tidiness very high on their list of priorities. They went into the kitchen and saw bits of food scattered everywhere, a couple of tins under the sink and the tap leaking, just like it had been when she had lived there.

They went upstairs, first into what had once been the bedroom she and Beryl had shared. Things had hardly changed. Her old bed was still there. So was the chest of drawers, the carpet full of holes and the mirror with a crack down one side. The last time she had looked in that mirror she had seen a thin spotty faced 18 year old. Now she was approaching 60 with a chubby face, and a nicely styled haircut with not the slightest strand of grey in it. One thing had not changed though. Her face was still covered with freckles, something that she had once hated, but wasn't at all bothered about now.

She looked out of the window expecting to see the gardens of the houses in Windermere Avenue, but they were no longer there. What she saw was the lawn of the Ashurst Housing Care Home. She turned to look at the wall above her old bed. Amazingly, there were still some of the photographs there that she had once stuck to it: David Whitefield, Dickie Valentine, Lonny Donegan, Jack Palance, Sal Mineo and William Holden she recognised. On the floor were a few more including those of Eddie Calvert, Gerry Marsden and John Wayne.

Alan had hardly said a word since they had entered the house and she was now feeling frightened. It was like something out of a dark Swedish film. She tugged at one of the drawers, it opened noisily and she saw a collection of children's clothes, clearly in need of a wash. She tugged at the second drawer. It was difficult to open, just like it had always been. She pushed it closed and turned round to discover that she was alone. Alan had disappeared.

She dashed into what had once been auntie Lil's bedroom. The tattered curtains were closed and it was dark. In the corner she thought she saw the back of auntie Lil holding something up to the wall. She looked up at the ceiling. It was so discoloured, stained by smoke for auntie Lil had been a heavy smoker all her life. She looked again at what she thought was auntie Lil, but this time saw it was an old frock on a coat hanger.

Was auntie Lil suddenly going to reappear? Maybe she would ask for the rent that Thelma had not paid her for the last 40 odd years. Then Thelma remembered that auntie Lil had died in the summer of 1963. Maybe someone else might now want the rent money from her. Alan would help her, wouldn't he, but where was he?

She dashed onto the landing and ran down the stairs. There was no sign of him there either. She tried to open the back door. She couldn't. It was locked. She tried the front door. She couldn't open that either. Had he locked her in? Why? Then she heard a loud bang. As she stood in the hall at the bottom of the stairs, she saw a bowl come tumbling down and smash onto the floor right in front of her.

"Alan, where are you? Where are you?"

"Here."

She looked up and saw him. A minute earlier he had been stood at the top of the stairs holding that bowl. It had slipped out of his hands and come crashing down. Everything was fine. Nothing was wrong. It had all been in her head, almost certainly for no more than a couple of minutes. Where had he just disappeared to? There was a simple explanation. He had gone into the bathroom for a call of nature.

They didn't stay much longer. Thelma now wanted to be as far away from the house as possible. They left and walked down Grasmere Avenue and onto Haydock Lane, where they saw the car waiting patiently to take them somewhere welcoming and safe.

On the way back he explained how he had managed to get hold of the key. The Council were about to demolish all the houses in Grasmere Avenue. Most of those in Keswick Avenue and Cumberland Avenue had already gone. The paperwork about their demolition was being handled by a woman who once lived opposite Alan in Chisnall Avenue. She knew where Thelma had once lived and thought that they both might like to have one last look at it. So she had lent him the key to the house and told him that the most recent tenants had been a Polish family, who had just left the country to return to their home town of Gdansk.

To help her get over what he now realised had been a bad experience, Alan decided they would go up to Burtonwood to see Rebecca. By the end of the evening Thelma was back to her usual self. There they had spent much of the time there discussing the main news of the day, the invasion of Iraq that had just been launched. As a result Alan did not have any opportunity to tell her of the possibility of her going to Greece with him.

The next day when Alan returned home from work, the house was empty and Thelma was nowhere to be seen. A casserole dish was in the oven with a note on the table telling him to switch the oven on if she hadn't returned. Where was she? Where had she disappeared to?

Sometime later she appeared with a large smile on her face to tell him that she had just spent the last hour watching a gang of demolition men from Ellesmere Port demolish her old house. The place was now just a large heap of rubble and she felt a lot better for it. Then she told him how upset she had been the previous evening and how she started thinking that he was going to finish it all with her.

"Well I'm sorry about all that, Thelma. All I can do is tell you to listen to the words of the song *Blue Roses* by Jimmy Nail because that is still what I think about you and always will."

But before he could spell out the words, into the house came Robert and Megan and soon Thelma was telling them what had happened the previous day and then what auntie Lil had been like. She was a poor cook, smoked like a trooper, watched and snored through the most trashy programmes on the television, and had no great conversational skills. It was no doubt all related to how she had been brought up in Nook End, one of six children, not all of whom had had the same father. On top of all that she had been going deaf, but at least her heart had been in the right place for the way she had let Beryl and Thelma live with her had been a lifesaver for both teenage girls, as they were then.

Robert and Megan stayed for tea and then after they had left, Alan and Thelma watched *Channel Four News*. It was dominated by the main international event of the day, or maybe the main international event of the year, the invasion of Iraq by American, British and Polish forces. At around half past seven there was a knock on the door. It was Phil, carrying a large parcel. It was addressed to Thelma and had been delivered to his house earlier in the day. In it were some books that she had ordered. Phil then told them that he and his partner Janice were just about to open a bottle of wine to celebrate her birthday and would they like to join them?

Janice was quite an interesting character and had an unusual background. She had been born in Oldham just after the end of the war. At the age of eight her family had gone to live in South Africa. She could not remember much of her time there, mainly because they had not stayed long and had returned to England to settle on the Isle of Wight. They had only been there a few months when her father had been killed in a car accident and soon after her mother had brought Janice and her brother back to Oldham. Her mother later remarried to someone who had been a lovely man to them all, even more so when he introduced Janice to a young man from Salford who he worked with. Soon after, marriage had resulted, but sadly it came to an end when he had been killed in an accident at work. After being a widow for more than 15 years, she had met Phil in that pile up on the M62 and now she was a regular visitor to his house.

Alan knew that Janice worked for a firm in Manchester that traded in textiles and on a number of occasions she had attended exhibitions held in various cities right across Europe. One country he knew that she had visited was Greece, which gave him the opportunity to talk about his next trip abroad.

"How well do you know Athens, Janice? Do you think that it would be a nice place for a holiday?"

"Well, it is certainly a lot nicer than Ashurst. In fact I would say it is almost as beautiful as Oldham."

"When you were over there did you ever visit a town called Thrakomakedhones?"

She had, just once, but didn't remember much about the place.

"That is where Thelma's father came from."

Janice was immediately interested to know more, but before she could say anything more, Alan went on: "I might be going near there in a couple of weeks' time."

"When was that decided Alan? You've never mentioned it."

"I only found out about it yesterday and I haven't had the chance to tell you about it yet. Do you want to come with me? My old mate Winston has an apartment there. That's why I think we might also be able to visit Thrakomakedhones if you want to come with me."

Then, turning to Janice, Alan went on: "I bet Phil never surprises you with something like that, does he?"

Janice laughed.

"Well you are wrong there, Alan. This afternoon we decided that we have both had enough of travelling up and down the M62 to see each other, so I am going to let my son and his family live in my house at Hollinwood and I am going to move in here with Phil. That is the real reason why we asked you two to come round. We'd just like you to be the first to know that you've now got a very noisy, ill behaved, loud mouthed, nosey neighbour to put up with."

Among the various topics they later talked about was the invasion of Iraq, as it would have been discussed in many houses all across the land. And so by the time they were back in their own house, Thelma had forgotten everything about what had happened the previous day. On her mind now were two things, the rapidly changing situation in the Middle East and the prospect of a trip to Greece. What might she now be able to discover about her father? Maybe she should e-mail her cousin Laurie in Sydney again. She could ask him to try and find a little more out about him from some of the older Greeks who were still living around the Camperdown suburb of the city.

At the weekend, Phil hired a van and drove to Oldham with Alan to collect some of Janice's possessions. It would not have been possible to have brought all of them back. That would have required an Eddie Stobart lorry because Janice was a bit like Alan. She never liked to throw anything away. Among her great interests in life were collecting paintings and reading books about the lives of famous painters. Soon after her moving in with Phil, her interest moved on to painting every wall in his house, but then none of them had seen fresh paint since around the time of the Festival of Britain in 1951.

A few days later Alan came home to find his wife sitting in the living room heavily engrossed in reading a very large book: "Look what Janice has lent me. It's the history of the French impressionist school of painters."

"Well you have certainly made an impression on me since I first met you. Is there anything in it about that?"

As he walked into the kitchen he saw a large painting on the wall.

"What's this?"

"Do you like it? I think it's really relaxing to look at. It's a present from her as well. It's called *Springtime in Louveciennes*."

"And where might Louveciennes be?"

"It's where Camille Pissaro did some of his paintings."

"Obviously."

It was quite a nice painting, colourful, providing a feel of peace and relaxation, but it seemed quite out of place, certainly when hung over the fireplace, alongside a photograph of the St Helens Rugby League 1956 Challenge Cup team and a black and white photograph of Sir Herbert Walker KCB, a Patriot LMS steam locomotive pulling wagons out of Ashurst railway station on a winter's day in 1949.

There were more walls around the house to fill with paintings and photographs, Alan thought. He didn't think that the painting would be the only one their new neighbour would give or lend them. Janice had only been there for a short time, but had already made an impression on both of them, an impressionist's impression one might even say.

17. An evening in Bailiff Bridge

Sport played a very important part in the lives of Alan and many of his friends and workmates. For those who lived in Ashurst, their main sport was either rugby league or association football. Some people liked both; some liked one and maybe other sports as well. Some enjoyed a sport because they liked to play it, though not watch it, while others like to watch a sport, but had never played it. Quite a few older ones would like to talk about their favourite sport more as it used to be and not as it was now. That was certainly true of one old-timer from Helmsley who had followed Widnes for years. When News Corporation had offered £87 million to persuade the rugby league authorities to change from a winter to a summer game, he said that he had lost all interest in a game that he followed all his life.

One person who had changed her sporting habits over the years was Alan's cousin Marion. When she lived in Astley, she was a football fan and followed Crompton Recs who played in the Lancashire Combination, mainly because her brother had been their goalkeeper. On going to Hull University her interest in sport had switched to cross country running which she had taken up with much enthusiasm. After marrying a young man from Willerby, she went to live on a farm at the quaintly named Sunk Island and changed her interest in sport again, this time to training race horses.

Alan's first interest in sport had been watching the Saints and playing football for Astley United in the Ashurst under–19 League. On reaching the age limit, he had switched to playing rugby union for Wilkinson's Social Club. He usually played in either their second or third team, though on one occasion he had managed to reach the dizzy heights of the first XV. He would have preferred to play league, but at the time the company did not have a rugby league section. That was due to the attitude and general outlook of its then owner and managing director, Basil Wilkinson.

Right at the start of his third season, there had been a right bust up in the affairs of the rugby club. People did not have to work at Wilkinson's to be able to play for them. But those who did work there were always chosen in preference to those who didn't, which was fair enough. Other than that, it was fairly easy for any rugby player to get a game in the third team. Quite often on a Saturday afternoon, whenever any local amateur rugby league team did not have a game, various young men would call in to see if they could play. According to the hierarchy who ran rugby union at Twickenham, this was totally wrong. But nobody had ever complained about it until Mr Fairweather, one of Basil's old university chums had arrived on the scene. He had been recruited by Basil to take charge of a new department called Personnel.

Before coming up to Ashurst, Mr Fairweather had had experience of running a union club in Surrey. He was a stickler for the observance of rules and particularly those that dealt with that alien, barbaric northern sport of rugby league. With Basil's full blessing, he soon began to make his presence felt in the affairs of the Purple and Whites as the team was known. When 'Fairy' discovered who was being allowed to play for the club, he sent a note throughout the factory stating that anyone who had ever played rugby league before would now not even be permitted to enter the club's changing rooms.

With this clearly understood, the teams for the following Saturday's games had been chosen on the Thursday evening after training. Mr Fairweather had also told the captain that he would be travelling with them on the coach, along with his brother-in-law, who was up north for a few days and staying with his sister who lived on the Wirral. When the 41 seater coach arrived outside the Warrington Road gates, there were only eight people waiting to get on it. All those who should have been there, and weren't, had at some point in their lives played rugby league. None of them liked the way Mr Fairweather had taken over and most of those who were now barred had decided to go and watch the Saints play Huddersfield in the Challenge Cup instead.

This was something that amused many people who worked on the shop floor because Mr Fairweather had made few friends, but quite a few enemies, in the short time he had been around. On the tennis section notice board, one wag had even gone as far as to pin up a sheet of paper on which he had written "Anyone who has ever played badminton before will no longer be permitted to play tennis here."

As a result the club began to slide into decline. A few members, including the club captain, switched to playing league; others to playing football, some stayed with the XV-man code, but switched to St Helens Moss Lane or Vulcan, who played at nearby Newton-le-Willows. Alan and four of his mates decided to retire temporarily and start watching the Saints every week.

This had been in the 'Swinging Sixties', now some 40 years ago and with all the changes at work over the last few years, many of his old rugby mates no longer worked at the firm. Fortunately, there were still a few people with whom he could discuss the game. There was Cliff, of course. He was a former Knowsley Road schoolboy, who had grown up in Mulberry Avenue and had known the great Wigan centre Eric Ashton who lived nearby. Then there was Colin, who had been brought up on the other side of Billinge and was a strong Wigan fan, and the commissioning engineer Tony Griffiths. Tony was Ashurst born-and-bred, supported Warrington, but as he worked out on site for most of the time, conversations with him, were few and far apart

On the shop floor there were a couple more league fans, including Jack, who had once played a season with Rochdale Hornets in their 'A' team; Eric who lived at Collins Green and was a diehard Widnes fan; Maurice, the secretary of Helmsley Hornets and Tommy, a referee in Warrington. Despite being relatively few in number, there were always plenty of discussions about the game and also with the various technical sales reps who called in from time-to-time to show Alan their company's latest electrical products and devices.

Such a discussion occurred soon after, when a rep from a firm in Leeds had been their visitor. After he had given them information about his company's new products, he commented on a photograph of an old Saints legend that was pinned on the wall. It was the winger Tom van Vollenhoven and the rep went on to tell Alan that he used to follow Hunslet and had been at Odsal for the 1959 Championship Final against St Helens.

This led on to Alan outlining what he remembered about that particular game. He had travelled that morning with three of his mates along with two coach loads of supporters from Earlestown. They had met in a pub close to the railway station, where they had had a couple of pints, before trooping onto the waiting coaches. Alan had travelled in a different coach to the others. Some would say that wouldn't really matter as they would all meet up in the car park in a couple of hours' time. However, they did not meet up there, because the second coach did not get to the ground before half-time. Both coaches had travelled along the East Lancashire Road, gone through Oldham, over the top, dropped down into the West Riding and soon after that they were going through Brighouse. A mile further on Alan's coach went past a sign that stated they were now in Bailiff Bridge, with the second coach about three cars behind. Alan's coach went through the traffic lights and past Firth's large carpet mill on the right hand side, just as the lights had changed to red.

Their coach crawled slowly on for the traffic now was very heavy. As Odsal Stadium came into sight it was nearly quarter to three and behind them there was no sign of the second coach. They all got off the coach, walked quickly to the turnstiles and joined the enormous crowd already in the ground. There was hardly time to draw breath, look at the programme or anything else before the two teams began climbing down the steps from the dressing rooms and running onto the pitch. Hunslet went in front early on and it seemed as though they were going to win easily, but then came that short burst by Alan's boyhood hero, the centre Duggie Greenall. He drew the opposition, fed his winger and the rest was history.

That was not how all those travelling in the second coach saw it. Their coach had got held at the lights at Bailiff Bridge and only managed to get to Odsal at the end of the first half.

Then Colin chipped in with another tale about a big game at Odsal. It was one that involved his uncle and the Cup Final replay between Warrington and Halifax in 1954 when over 120,000 spectators had turned up. At the time, his uncle worked at the Thames Board Mills in Warrington. He had knocked off early that day and made the journey over the Pennines in a car with three workmates. There was no M62 motorway then and by the time they had reached Brighouse, traffic was down to a crawl. Half an hour after leaving the town centre, they had travelled less than a mile and had not quite got as far as Bailiff Bridge. At that point it was clear that they would get no nearer to Odsal, which was still a couple of miles further on.

The four of them got out of the car, stretched their legs as they wondered what to do next. At that point an old man had come out of a nearby house and asked them if they were from Warrington. He told them that they would never get to Odsal, but they were welcome to come into his front room and listen to the commentary on his wireless. They gratefully accepted his offer and within five minutes, the old man's wife had brought them cups of tea and a plateful of scones that she had just baked.

While they were waiting for the commentary to start, one of the Warrington lads asked the man if they were anywhere near a place called Shelf.

"Aye, it's a couple of miles away, on the outskirts of Bradford. Why?"

"I was in the Navy during the war and a good pal of mine was on the same ships as me, the Phoenix first and then the Waverley. I often wonder what happened to him. All I know of him was that he lived at Shelf and was a keen Crown Green bowler."

"What was his name?"

"It was a bit of a funny name. Lightowler. I'd never heard anybody called that before. Tommy Lightowler, that was his name, but we all used to call him Tommy Lighthouse. He was an ace guy."

"Lightowler is a fairly common name in Bradford."

At this point the man's wife went out of the room and returned a few minutes later, holding a photograph in her hand.

"Is that him?"

"Yes. Well blow me down, after all these years. How is the old bugger? I'd love to meet him again. How come you have you got this? Is he one of your relatives?"

"Well he was. He was my older brother. He died last year."

"Oh, I am sorry."

And then the Warrington man spoke well of Tommy, someone who it had been his privilege to have known and to have fought on the same side as in the war against Fascism.

Then the rep told a tale about the same game. At the time he had been working at Ferranti Transformers at Hollinwood in Oldham. A group of his workmates decided that they fancied going to the game. They knocked off at lunch time and went up to the lad's house where his dad was going to let them use his car. The house was on the main road heading east out of Oldham town centre. They all got into the car which was parked on the drive and the driver had edged forward off the drive, onto the pavement, but then could go no further. His way was blocked by a lorry. In front of the lorry all they could see were more cars. Behind the lorry all that they could see were more cars. The bulk of the traffic was probably all going to the match and for a game in Bradford in West Yorkshire over 30 miles away and starting in around four hours' time.

Despite this, they still managed to arrive at Odsal with about 10 minutes to spare. They hurried to the turnstiles and joined a long queue. The driver was in front of the other three. He handed over his money at the turnstile and while he was waiting for his change from a pound note, the pressure outside on the wooden block housing six turnstiles finally caused them to collapse and the others got in for free, as did many hundreds if not thousands of others. Whether they saw much of that match was doubtful though. With such a large crowd there, it was unlikely that many people had a good view of all the action.

Later that afternoon Alan thought again about his trip to Odsal in 1959 and about Geoff, Ken and Paul, his three mates who he should have travelled on the same coach with, but didn't. He had seen them on the following night in the Raven and heard their tale of woe. He had seen them regularly over the next four or five years too, but slowly they all lost contact with each other. It was nothing deliberate, just what used to happen to one time best mates.

That evening he flicked through the pages of the *Ashurst Star*. It never had much topical or interesting news in it. The paper was all right for those who wanted to buy or sell a house, or were looking for a tradesman to do something that you couldn't do yourself or to inform the readers about who had recently died and been buried in Windle Steps Cemetery.

But it wasn't much good for real news, well not usually, but there was one story in this week's edition that interested him. It was about a woman called Joan Mills, who had been in his first class at Lane Head School. She had lived in Ashurst until 1948 when her family had emigrated to New Zealand. Now she was back in England to promote a book she had written about the threat to the environment by global warming. He remembered her well because she had always chosen him in the country dancing lesson that Miss Travis always ran. In addition, on her sixth birthday, someone had dared her to kiss a boy and she had chosen him. Little things really, but they had made an impression on him and now she going to give a talk in Bolton Lane Library. What a pity it was going to clash with a trip he had to make to Aberthaw Power Station.

Then he read the other free weekly paper, the *Ashurst Reporter*. The main story concerned another old school friend, Roger Price.

When they were about 10 years old, they had both been keen train spotters and had remained so for quite a long time after. In Alan's case that had been until he was around 20 years old. In Roger's case, it was still ongoing. The reason for the paper's interest in Roger was that he had just returned from a week in Hungary with a group of local railway enthusiasts. Among the places they had visited was the engine sheds at Gyor, about two miles from the Rabatext Cotton Mill that Alan had once visited a few years ago.

Another page of general interest was number seven, the 'road to heaven' page. Often there were names of people he knew. This time the paper reported the death of John Foulkes. He had once played football with Alan for Astley United and among the mourners were Mr and Mrs Hunwick, who still lived in Chisnall Avenue, a couple who he knew well.

The Reporter always carried more adverts than news and this sometimes led to some stories being spread over two pages or sometime placed in a poor position. No more so than in this issue where alongside all the funerals was a piece about a couple from Huyton who had been charged with running a brothel at Nook End.

If that was funny in an odd sort of way, there was nothing funny about the other story that he read. It was about a young man from Warwick Street who had been killed in Iraq, someone by the name of John Greenall. He was not a relative, he was not even known to Alan, but he was an Ashurst lad, whose family would now be mourning his death.

121

18. The good Yorkshireman

Alan was late home from work. He had driven Tariq to the garage on Bolton Lane where his car was being repaired. However, when he arrived home, it didn't matter because he was greeted with the news that their tea would be late. Rebecca had been round earlier with the children and had stayed longer than she had planned. It wouldn't be the first time that had happened. The tea was still cooking in the oven and Thelma was sat watching the news, with the main story being about the ever worsening situation in the Middle East. As they listened to the various reporters, the phone rang. Thelma answered it and took it into the kitchen. After a few minutes she returned with tears in her eyes.

"Alan, that was Joyce. She told me that Sam died this morning."

Samuel John Holroyd was born in Egypt in 1920. A few weeks later his parents had taken him and his older brother to Dunkirk. Those with a good knowledge of world geography might feel that that needed some clarification or explanation. In fact it was quite a short move. Egypt is located high up above Queensbury between the city of Bradford and the town of Halifax. Dunkirk is a district of Halifax and not too far from another spot with a quaint and foreign sounding name, Mount Tabor.

At the age of 18, a few months before the outbreak of the Second World War, Sam had joined the Merchant Navy. In the spring of 1947 he had married Joyce, and started work at Wilkinson's. Within a couple of years he had joined the Drawing Office. By the time Alan had arrived there, he had also become the stepfather of Maureen, the daughter of Joyce's sister and her husband after they had both been tragically killed in a motorbike accident at Burtonwood.

For all the time they had worked together in the Drawing Office, Sam had been the only Yorkshireman in the place. He had taken much stick over the years for that mortal sin, but had always given as good as he got. He had retired in 1985. Recently, Thelma had noticed his decline each time they had visited and now she was the first person outside his family to know that he was no longer with them.

During their short conversation, Thelma asked Joyce whether she wanted them to come up to see her. She did and so an hour later, they found themselves knocking on the front door of the house that

Joyce had lived in since 1941. Both Thelma and Alan felt sad, but Joyce looked quite happy as she ushered her two visitors into the kitchen. On the table was a bottle of rum, Sam's favourite drink, three glasses and a bottle of stilled water. Joyce filled the three glasses, passed the one with just water in it to Thelma saying what she always said to her best friend: "I know that you'll be driving."

Then they all clinked their glasses and drank a toast: "To Sam."

"To Sam"

"To Sam."

"So how are you, Joyce? I feel terrible about it."

"I'm fine, Thelma. I really am. You see Sam may have stopped breathing this morning, but in reality he left us three or four weeks ago. He wasn't the same man I had known for the last 50 years. So his death didn't come as a complete shock. In fact, it came as a relief to us, and to Paul and Maureen too, although the grandchildren can't yet fully understand what's happened to him."

She took a large swig from her glass, refilled it and went on: "You see, I have lived with Sam since 1947 and I think I have enjoyed every day of it with him. He was always good and interesting to talk to and talk with. He was a wonderful dad to Paul and then to Maureen after her parents were killed. We shared so much together, the pair of us, but over the last month I knew it was all finished so I am glad he's gone. I had to do everything for him and I knew he hated it too."

She took another swig from her glass and continued: "When I look back at my life, I realise how lucky I've been, having my parents, my brother and sister, neighbours I've had, friends, knowing you two. Maybe not my first husband, but things were different then what with the war and all that. And then last Monday when I was out shopping and I heard what happened to a young lass up at Nook End."

At that point the phone rang. She spoke on it for a minute, then slammed it down: "What do I want with a new kitchen?"

Then she continued with her tale: "I think her name is Chantelle, anyway they only got married at the end of December. Her husband had joined the Army about six months ago. He had been out of work for over a year. I don't think he had ever had a proper job. They had no money and she was expecting their first child. You could say that he was forced into it really. Anyway she learnt yesterday he was coming home which meant he would be here for the birth. But not all of him was coming home. He was badly injured in a bomb blast in Baghdad in the first few days of the war and lost both his legs and they think he has suffered brain damage as well. What sort of a life will that be for the pair of them? Maybe when she is as old as me, how many happy memories will she have? I've got so many."

The person Joyce had just spoken of was not the only soldier from Ashurst to have been hurt or killed and the war had only been going on for less than a month.

"You see it was all different with the Second World War. We knew what we were fighting against. Hitler, the Nazis, Fascism and all that went with it. What are we fighting for in Iraq? The Americans want the oil; that is what all this war is about. How many people lost their lives in that war Iraq had with Iran? Probably tens of thousands and how many British lads will come home in coffins or will come home to a life like Chantelle's husband will now have?"

She took another swig from her glass, emptied it, stood up and put it in the sink, sat down and said: "Don't worry about me. I'll be fine. I'll be glad when we've buried him. I'll still have my memories, my friends and especially you two."

She stood up again, hugged the pair of them and continued: "I'm not going to drink any more. I want to show you a few things."

She went upstairs and returned carrying a photograph album and a shoe box. She opened the album first. In it were photographs from Sam's early life. There were a few from his time growing up in Mytholmroyd, his parents, his school, a dog, the Piece Hall in Halifax and their wedding photographs, Joyce pointing out all the faces and names and the fact that the only people still alive now were probably her and her son Paul.

Then she picked out a larger one showing a group of men standing outside Wilkinson's main gates on Warrington Road. It included Sam, Charlie, Mick, from Platt Bridge and right at the back was Alan.

"I remember that day" Alan said. "It was a two hour strike the union called for when Basil said DATA could only represent draughtsmen and none of those who worked in the Metal Fatigue Lab or the Wages Department. We had only been out for a short time when Basil sent a message to tell Len to come to his office in and have an informal chat about the situation. So Len sent a message back to say that he would come on condition that he brought a member of the Office Committee with him. Basil agreed and so Len took a fellow called Henry with him. He worked in the lab, but when Basil saw him, he said Henry could not come into his office because that would prejudice the talks. So Len suggested that he came into the office to discuss how to get everybody back to work, but that the office door be left open with Henry standing outside. It was farcical really, but Basil agreed and finally accepted that DATA could represent all its members, even those who were not draughtsmen."

Then Alan pointed to various other people on the photograph and talked about what had happened to all those that he knew about.

"Quite a few names you've mentioned there Alan I can remember Sam talking about. You see every night when he came home, he would tell me what had happened at work that day. At first it was all about Charlie and Mick and Alan Groves the section leader. Then he got to know you, Len and Stan, the one who took part in the liberation of Belsen."

She picked up the photograph again, looked at it, then put it down and carried on: "I remember when he first got to know you. He used to tell me that you were a nice lad, but a bit gullible and then when you got involved with that petition to keep the station open, well Sam was really impressed with what you were doing."

The phone rang again. It was the sister of one of Sam's old ship mates to tell him that another old timer called Ben had died and that his funeral would be at Pontefract in three days' time.

"I'm sorry to hear your news, but I am afraid that Sam will not be able to come. He's going to his own funeral that day."

Then she carried on reminiscing: "I remember the first time that I ever saw you, Thelma. It was at the works dance, the one they had at the Floral Hall in Southport. I was going into the cloakroom to leave my coat there. A young girl in front of me held the door for me and then I saw another young girl with a face full of freckles coming the other way. I thought to myself 'I wonder if that was Alan's girlfriend' because Sam always liked to call you 'Freckles' when he was talking about you."

Then Thelma spoke about the first time she could remember meeting Joyce: "I think that the first time I ever saw you, was when we were both in Woolworths one Saturday morning. You were in there shopping with Sam."

"That's right and I felt really rude because Sam wanted to stop and talk and I was wanting to get home and put the dinner on as we were going out again in the afternoon. So I hope you'll forgive my bad behaviour."

They both laughed.

"So when is the funeral, Joyce?"

"Probably next Monday. I'm waiting for the Co-op to ring back."

"Will you get any divi?" laughed Alan.

"Have you got any plans for the future if you don't mind me asking?"

"Of course I don't mind you asking Thelma. You are my best friend and if I ever need any help or someone to talk to, I know where you both live and I know I can rely on you."

They both nodded.

"Now there are couple of things I do want you to help me with."

"What are they?"

"The first thing is for you Alan. Can you go and tell Charlie what's happened?"

"Yes, no problem."

"And tell him in the nicest possible way that I don't expect him to come to the funeral. I know he's not been well for a long time."

"Sure, and what's the other thing?"

"It's for you Thelma. How much would you charge to teach me how to use a computer?"

"A penny a go, but for that you'll get a Welsh scone and a glass of Pernod too. So are you going to get one?"

"If I like doing it, yes. I know you can do it and a lot of people that are my age seem to enjoy it as well."

Then Alan chipped said: "It's very addictive. I know a couple of people at work who probably spend three or four hours a night on it."

Alan had a couple of websites he looked at most evenings, mainly the rugby league ones, rlfans.com, totalrl.com and the Red Vee. Another site he often visited was the St Helens Connect site. One of the most interesting things about this site was the Genealogy section. This provided information about the births, marriages and deaths of local people not just in the town, but from all round the area.

One side of Alan's family originally lived in Fingerpost in St Helens. It was where his granddad had been born and spent his first seven years until the family had moved to Ashurst on the last day of the 19th century. As far as Alan knew, all of his granny's side of the family had been born in Ashurst, although he did know that one of her uncles had moved to Widnes around 1925 to be near to the sea.

"Would you be interested in doing your family tree, Joyce?"

"I think I might. Would I be able to do Sam's as well? Will that be on it somewhere?"

Alan laughed: "You will be absolutely amazed just how much information is available and going back years and years and years. In fact last week I discovered some information about Moses on it."

"Really," said Joyce not quite believing what she had just heard.

"He means Glyn Moses, a Welshman who used to play full-back for the Saints."

Then Thelma continued with Joyce's introduction to the World Wide Web: "When Alan told me about the St Helens Connect site, I tried to find out if there was a similar site in Tonyrefail or any towns near to it in South Wales. I thought that I might be able to find out a bit about my mother or her family but I've had no luck yet."

"There's another thing I am going to get started on as well, something that I have wanted to do for years. Painting, and not just me painting on a board and easel. I'm also interested in their lives, you know reading about them and what inspired them to paint. Maybe I might start going to classes again. I used to go to one a long time ago."

"The partner of our next door neighbour, Phil, is a painter and a collector too. We'll have to get you to meet her. Her name is Janice, she's just a bit younger than me."

"I am also going to join this anti-war campaign. I got a leaflet from a young girl handing them out outside ASDA last Saturday. And I am going to join Astley Pensioners' Club too. I know a widow from Astley who goes there every week and she thinks it's wonderful what they do."

The phone rang again. It was another person passing on their condolences, another old age pensioner who sounded very sad and totally sober, listening to Joyce, now slightly inebriated and quite lively as well.

"That was another of his old ship mates from Redcar. News travels fast doesn't it?"

As they drove back home, Thelma asked Alan how well did he think Joyce was coping with her sad loss.

"I think she'll be all right. She's got Paul, Maureen, the grandchildren and us two as well. We've got to help her though without it appearing that we are interfering too much. It's a good thing that she is going to start coming round here for some computer lessons. But take it easy with her, don't rush her. When she comes, get her to stay for a meal as well. I'm sure that she'll appreciate it."

Yes, it was sad that Sam had died, but it was good the way that his widow was looking forward to making a fresh start to her life. Their last few weeks together had not been very nice for Joyce or Sam, but now Joyce's future was what mattered most.

The funeral was held in Ashurst Parish Church. Neither Sam nor Joyce were religious, but that place seemed the most appropriate. It was there where the funeral of Joyce's sister and husband had taken place a long time ago.

There must have been nearly 100 people in the church. Sam had been well liked by just about everybody he had come into contact with. There were even two car loads that had driven over from the West Riding to pay their respects, including one old man who had been at school with Sam's older brother, a sergeant in the Green Howards, who had been killed during the Normandy landings in 1944.

Yes, Sam would be greatly missed by everybody who had known him. He had been one of the best. He had been a good husband, a good father and a good friend to almost everybody who had ever known him. He had fought in the war against fascism, he had been a good trade union member and much more too. The day he had drawn his last breath was a day that the world became that little bit poorer.

19. The Bolton wanderer

The following day, a number of people who worked in different parts of the factory asked Alan to pass on their condolences to Sam's widow. Everyone who did spoke well of him and invariably used the phrase "I remember when he did this" or "I'll always remember him for this, that or whatever". Over the next few days, as the news went round, other former workmates rang Alan with the same message and so one of Yorkshire's finest exports into Lancashire was mentioned in many conversations around the town.

A few old timers apologised to Alan for the fact that much as they would have liked to, they could not attend Sam's funeral. Ron Dalton was now living in Southport and caring for a sick wife; Jack Hill was domiciled at Withernsea on the east coast of Yorkshire and hating every minute of it; and Les Fishwick lived in a large Victorian house on Hardmans Lane directly opposite the entrance to Windle Steps Cemetery. But now he rarely moved out of his bedroom and certainly never got as far as the pavement outside his house. If Alan told him the day of the funeral and the time the hearse would be going into the cemetery, Les would stand at his window and pay his respects to his old Yorkshire pal.

In the end, almost 100 people did attend the funeral, but by the following Tuesday things in the Drawing Office had moved on.

"So what did you do over this long weekend Cliff? Anything that is highly embarrassing or something that you don't want anybody to know about?"

"Well if I did do something that was highly embarrassing or something that I didn't want anybody to know about, why would I tell you?"

Normally things ran quite smoothly in the Platt household, but on the Friday evening his son John had come round to tell his parents that his girlfriend Fiona had walked out on him. They had lived together for over a year and he was completely shocked by what she had done, for it had come right out of the blue. Now he would no longer be able to afford to live in the house on his own and might even have to revert to being 'The Bolton wanderer'.

He had acquired that nickname a few years ago. On leaving Ashurst Comprehensive, he had enrolled on a course at Bolton

Technical College. It wasn't really that far to go there every day from Ashurst, but after a while he accepted an offer of accommodation that he couldn't refuse. A fellow student had decided that neither the subject he was studying nor the town that he was studying it in, were for him and so he had gone back home to Brighton. As a result there was a spare room in the house on Blackburn Road where Miles had lived along with four others. One was Joe, another was Frank and the other two he had hardly spoken to. When John went round to see the place, he discovered that Joe was actually Josephine, Frank was Frances, and the other two were also girls. Paula had been in his class at Ashurst Comprehensive and the fourth was a Spanish girl with long hair and a long name to go with it.

John moved in the next night and lived there until Christmas when a dispute with the landlord led to them all moving a couple of hundred yards away. He stayed there until the beginning of the second year, by which time he and Josephine had moved into another shared house in Breightmet. This went on for a while until they had decided to rent a cottage together at Astley Bridge. This lasted for almost a year, until she decided to end their relationship and go back home to Aberdeen. For the rest of his student days he lived first at Little Lever, then at Blackrod, finally finishing up in a squat on Manchester Road. Hence his nickname, 'the Bolton wanderer'.

"He's going to have to come back home while he gets himself sorted out. To be honest I'm glad she's left him. A right little peas above sticks she was."

"What?"

"Peas above sticks. Have you never heard that one before? It means getting above your station. A stuck up little get, in ruder language."

"Didn't you like her then?"

"Well, what do you think?"

"I think that you didn't like her."

Things were quiet in the Drawing Office for the rest of the week. It was due to a combination of three things: Sam's death, Cliff's problems at home and Mr Musgrove's frequent visits. But then the boss went on holiday for a week and John's situation took a turn for the better, helped in a strange way by the death of his uncle Keith.

John's mother was the only relative left on her side of the family and so all his uncle's possessions went to her including his house in Penketh. It would be just the place for John to move into. Near enough though for him to call in for the odd meal and have all his washing done as well, no doubt.

So now Alan's son Robert and Cliff's son John both had a Warrington address. Yet another bit of a coincidence, which led to Alan thinking about his old mate Charlie and decide to go and visit him. The day after Sam had died he had rung Charlie, but without success. He had then rung Charlie's son Paul who told him that his dad had gone to stay for a few days with a relative in Fleetwood. But now he was back home and it would be a good time to visit him.

The pair of them went on the Thursday evening and found Charlie in his back garden, spade in one hand and a bunch of flowers in the other. When he saw them, they could see he hadn't changed a bit.

"I'm on gardening leave, did you not know, but I can start on Monday morning if that's why you have come to see me."

They all went back into the house and into his front room. He made them a drink, brought out a plate of cakes, put them on the table, then stroked his bookcase very lovingly and told them that the former Saints hooker, Bob Dagnall, had made it for him. Then he sat down and talked about his holiday on the Fylde coast.

It was over 10 minutes before either of them could get a word in. He certainly seemed to have enjoyed his time away, maybe because he had spent most of it bowling, something which he was still very good at. Finally he apologised for talking so much, jokingly said the holiday had been with a gang of Trappist monks before asking Thelma how she was. So it was quite some time before Alan could tell him about the death of his old mate Sam.

"Another one gone. They're all going and leaving me here on my own. There'll be no room for me up there when I go. Even my old pal Albert from Nutgrove went last week while I was away and he was only 79."

Then he asked about some of the people who still worked at Wilkinson's, what Alan thought about the current Saints team, enquired about Rebecca and Robert and asked whether Thelma had learned to speak Welsh yet.

Then he looked her closely in the face and said: "I think that you have lost some of your freckles. Are you using carbolic soap now?"

131

Before she could reply he went on: "Do you still go everywhere with that old shoulder bag you used to have, the one with that Ban the Bomb symbol on it and that thin green coat. How you kept warm in that, I'll never know."

Same old Charlie, what a loveable old guy he was. She had liked him from the very first time he had spoken to her.

Then he asked: "Do either of you two know what happened to Mick? Is he still living in Platt Bridge?"

"Charlie, he died in 1991. Have you forgotten? I thought you went to his funeral."

"He's died has he? Well he never told me. But then you know what Wiganers are like."

Then he carried on: "He used make me laugh did Mick. He was a top guy that lad, one of the best. I wonder if Sam's met him yet. Once they get going, they'll be plotting summat for me when I get up there. I'm sure of it. Still the place will be full of Saints won't it and I don't think Mick will like that very much, will he?"

Then, for no good reason, he proceeded to retell a story about Mick and Hazel, their old tea girl who had gone to Bradford College in 1975 with the aim of becoming a teacher. She had managed to work during the summer holidays, pushing a tea trolley round for the morning tea break and then doling out the chips in the canteen at lunchtime. During her first week back she had been telling her old workmates a bit about what life was like in Bradford and then she went on to say something that at first surprised them all: "By the way, I'm sure that you will all be interested to hear that I am now expecting."

Everybody assumed that meant that she was pregnant. Then she smiled and continued the sentence: "Yes, before we go back to college in September, I am expecting to go to India with my friend Sirindar. She's from Mysore in Hydrabad."

Mick had then replied with one of his absolutely classic retorts: "Tha'll be bloody mysore if tha starts having vindaloo for thi brekki every day. Tha'd better start nicking some toilet rolls now from t' stores."

Then Charlie reminded Alan of another incident involving their favourite Wiganer. He had returned from a visit to the Iron Foundry and as he sat down he said out loud for all to hear: "What's wrong

132

with Thelma? I think that she might be suffering from brain damage." You jumped up Alan and asked what had happened to her, had she been in an accident?

"Mick said: 'I've heard she started watching the Saints. She must be easily entertained.'

"Then I said to him: 'Mick, you're a typical Wiganer. What do you lot know about brain damage? You don't have any brains.' Well, it's true, Wiganers don't have any brains."

"You're wrong there Charlie. What about Chris Joynt, Sean Long, Dave Lyon, Bill Bretherton, Bill Sayer and Gus O'Donnell to name six that I can think of straightaway. They are all Wiganers."

"Only joking."

Then he carried on: "It's a good job we can have a bit of banter between us, isn't it. You wouldn't get that in soccer."

Then Charlie changed the subject and said to Thelma: "What do you think about this Labour Government, eh? Not much eh. I can't stand 'em. A load of men in suits who've never had a proper job in their lives. I bet our old MP, Leslie Spriggs, would turn in his grave if he saw how Tony Blair carries on. And St Helens has got a millionaire for an MP now. You couldn't make it up, could you? He's even got a butler. I mean he might be a nice bloke, but what can he know about how ordinary people live? I bet you never see him waiting for a bus or having trouble paying his electric bill."

While he paused for breath, Thelma managed to tell him that Sam's widow Joyce had sent her regards and was so glad that Sam had had such a good mate in Charlie.

"I know he was from Yorkshire, and we used to take the piss out of him summat rotten, but at the end of the day he was one of us. A good trade union man as well, he'd fought in the war and he could give it as well as tek it. You couldn't fault him. We were lucky to have him with us for so long. I hope she manages on her own."

"We'll keep an eye on her, Charlie. She's going to learn how to use a computer, she's going to start doing her family tree and she's going to start painting as well, which she tells us she has always been interested in."

"Well, she can come and paint my shed if she wants to. Our Paul keeps saying he will, but I'm not holding my breath."

"Are you still watching the Saints?"

"Oh aye. I don't watch them away so much now, but I go to every home game. As you know I didn't take to this Super League business and playing in the summer at first, but I think I do now. It's a lot faster than when I first started watching them. The handrags, that's what we use to call the Saints when I first went. Do you still go Thelma? Who are your favourite players?"

"I go to most home games, Charlie. As for my favourite players well I suppose it will be between something like Darren Albert, Paul Wellens, Kieron and Scully."

"Not a bad choice, but I bet you would have loved watching van Vollenhoven. He was sheer class that man, watching him was worth the entrance money alone. Did you see him when we beat Hunslet in that Championship Final? I did. I was there. Were you?"

Of course she hadn't been to that game. At the time she probably didn't even know where Ashurst or St Helens or Odsal Stadium were and her first game had been in 1963, some four years later.

"I remember you going to that game against Oldham and I remember you telling me that your favourite player then was Wilf Smith. Well you'll be pleased to know he's still going strong. I often see him when I'm stood selling the *Big Issue* on Elephant Lane."

The conversation carried on in a similar vein for over half an hour. Charlie just went on and on about things from the past, how he knew Alex Murphy, Austin Rhodes and Bob Dagnall and also an up-and-coming comedian Johnny Vegas although he had always known him as Michael Pennington when he was still at school. Then he started going back in time, telling Thelma how Elephant Lane and Donkey Common had got their names and how he and a whole load of his neighbours had once dug a train out of the snow at Thatto Heath station. Then he talked about how his dad had once worked in the boiler house at the asylum at Rainhill, but had left after six months because most of his work mates were driving him mad.

"If it had been built a bit nearer to Thatto Heath, do you know what its address would have been, eh? Nutgrove Road. An asylum on Nutgrove Road, eh. Mind you, where we lived in Emily Street was a bit mad, well it was with the family we had next door to us. Five kids and three parents lived there. Mad it was in there."

Soon it was time to leave. Charlie had clearly enjoyed himself having old friends to visit. Maybe it was just talking about the past that had cheered him up. He had many a good tale to tell, but then he always did have. Now he wasn't quite in full control of things, particularly when as they stood up to leave, he pointed to the bookcase and told them yet again what a fine joiner Bob Dagnall was and how he used to do a lot of work for a Countess down in London.

Alan didn't know that, maybe Charlie was making things up because it did seem a little unlikely, but Bob was a very good joiner.

"You'll come again won't you?" were his parting words to them. "But don't come tomorrow. I'm going out for me supper after I've finished bowling."

And before they could say anything in reply, he had slammed the front door shut.

The following day at lunch time Pete Mulholland asked Alan if he had been up to see Charlie the previous evening.

"Yes, how did you know?"

"I was at the top of Stafford Road waiting to get on to Prescot Road when you and Thelma drove past. How is he?"

"To be honest, I think he's losing it a bit. Just some of the things he said to us didn't seem quite right."

"It's funny you should say that because I've seen him twice in the last month and that's what I wondered."

"Where have you seen him then?"

"The first time was when I was getting out of the car outside our Janet's house in Scholes Lane. He was walking past on the other side of the road. I waved to him and shouted to him and he just blanked me. I couldn't believe it. The second time was in Wilkinson's DIY in Baldwin Street last week. There weren't many people in there and he was just mooching round. I went up to him, tapped him on the shoulder, asked him how he was and he told me to leave him alone. I told him I used to work with him at Wilkinson's. 'Not in here you didn't' he said and then off he went. I couldn't believe it. We were such good pals for years."

"Well he seemed fine for most of the time when we were with him, but then he is 83; so I know what you mean."

A short while later Alan asked Cliff if his son John was still living at home.

"No. Not now. He stayed with us for a bit while we cleaned uncle Keith's old house up. Then John bought himself a fridge, washing machine, TV and a few other things and we got him a new bed and some other bits and pieces. Last night he was on the phone to his mother telling her that everything was fine except for just one thing. Did she have the receipt for the new bed we had bought him? It would have to go back. It wasn't big enough. Now our Maud keeps receipts for anything she buys for at least five years so that was no problem. But what was the problem with the bed, she asked."

"What had happened was that on his second night there, he had gone shopping in the Co-op. Who should he see working on the tills but Paula, one of the girls who used to live in one of those Bolton houses he had once lived in. He told her where he was now living and invited her to come and see him sometime. She took up his offer straightaway. She told him she was finishing work in half an hour and so he waited for her. I think that they might have had a bit more than just a drink of coffee together. And now she has moved in with him."

"Lucky him."

"Well she's very much nicer than Fiona, the little thief."

"So where is this Paula from?"

"She grew up in Haresfinch, but her dad died in an accident down the pit when she was quite young and she and her mother moved to Hemsley. When she was 18 she went to live in Bolton when she was at Bolton Tech. From what our John says, she is really nice so we'll just have to wait and see how things work out for the pair of them."

20. "The spoilt papers might win it."

As Alan drove into work the following day, he recalled what had happened exactly 47 years ago in September 1955. It had been the occasion of his first day as an apprentice. He remembered clearly what he heard the Apprentice Training Officer, Jack Critchley making a very profound statement to him and the rest of the 20 young men who made up that year's group of new apprentices.

"Today is the first day in the rest of your lives."

Alan often wondered what had happened to all the others. He knew that one had left before the first Christmas but not why, one had been killed in an accident in the Iron Foundry, three had moved on to pastures new on coming out of their time and over the next 40 years, the others either gone to work at other firms, been made redundant, retired early or had died. Alan was the last one still working there and among his possessions he still had a copy of his first wage slip. It showed that he had received the grand sum of £4//13/6d.

From time-to-time, he had bumped into other members of that original group. Some had changed a lot, some hardly a bit. Some had done well in one way or another, some had had a raw deal or just been unlucky in life.

As he walked into his office, he saw a note on his desk from Mr Musgrove reminding him to make sure that all his section were assembled in the meeting room at 10am. Well he knew that Colin wouldn't be there as he had gone to Fiddlers' Ferry Power Station straight from home.

At the appointed hour, everybody except for Colin and Mr Musgrove were sitting around the large meeting room table. Among those present were Dave Morris and Tony Griffiths, both of whom could easily have been working somewhere miles away, maybe even abroad. Their presence indicated that clearly something important was on Mr Musgrove's agenda.

Ten minutes later, Tony stood up, looked at his watch, banged on the table and said in a very formal voice: "I hereby declare this meeting open. Do we have any apologies?"

"Mr Musgrove, I presume."

"Thank you Dave. If that is the case then I hereby suggest that we move onto the main item on the agenda which is Any Other Business."

"If you are running this meeting doesn't that mean Any Other Funny Business?" said Alan.

"One thing that we could discuss would be what time we can start eating today's buffet" said Cliff.

Whenever Mr Musgrove organised a meeting, he would always arrange for a buffet to be laid on, particularly if it included people who had come from outside the factory.

"Since Tony has just elected himself as chairman, why doesn't he start this meeting by telling us about some of the places that he has visited recently? I'm sure we would all learn a lot from all the jaunts that he has been on over the last few weeks."

"What a wonderful suggestion that is Dave, and after I have done that, perhaps you could tell us a bit about what sort of work you appear to be doing quite often at night in Ramsbottom."

They all laughed. Dave's little secret had never really been a secret to most of those present.

Tony sat down, coughed in a very important way and started on what might just be one of his regular performances: "Well, before I tell you where I have been recently, I think that I'll have to tell you a little bit about some of the places that I haven't been to recently."

There was silence, an indication that none of those present objected to his proposal.

"Well for a start I have not been in Cahoots. Apparently you can't go there alone. You can only go there with another person and there's nobody here that I would want to go away with. Another place I have not been is Cognito. I hear that no one ever recognises you when you are there and I always like to get on with folk, present company excepted. Neither have I ever been in Flexible. When you are there you always have to stick to what you want and not be accommodating and helpful like I always am.

"As regards places I have been to, well I liked it when I was in Suspense. It's one of my favourite places. It really gets the adrenalin flowing and pumps up the old heart. At my age I need all the stimuli that I can get. I have also been in Doubt. It's a really sad place to go to particularly if there is something that you are not sure about.

"During the last couple of months I have also been in Capable.

That's probably an age thing too. That is why you will never find me in Conclusion. The trouble is you have to jump to it and I'm not into much physical activity if I can help it.

"I've also been in Ramsbottom a couple of times as well although I have never stayed the night there. I hear that it is a place where you can never get a good night's rest."

Everybody laughed, then went quiet as Tony continued: "I was in Leigh last week. I had my dinner in that café on Railway Road. When I came out, there had been an accident right outside it. An ambulance man was attending to this woman lying on the pavement, in a right sorry state she was. I heard him say to her 'Where are you bleeding from, love?' She says 'I'm from Atherton, where are you bleeding from?'

"I was also up in Newcastle on a job a month ago with Billy Fairclough. On the first day after we had finished work, we went looking for somewhere to eat. We walked past this right seedy looking place behind the bus station and a bloke outside pointed to the door and said 'Come in here, lads. For £10 each, you can have a pie, a pint and the company of a nice young lady'.

"Billy says 'Whose pies are they?'

"He loves his food does Billy and in large quantities too. In the digs the following morning we had breakfast, porridge, egg and bacon and then a couple rounds of toast with a very small portion of honey. When we were checking out, Billy says to the landlady: 'I see that you keep a bee.'

"Now then, moving on, can I ask if any of you ever read our wonderful local paper? You should do, there is some good stuff in it, particularly if you are looking for a bit of romance."

Silence.

"Well then here's a few that I can remember reading in last Friday's paper:

Lady from Sale who is not for sale and likes animals, seeks a man who does not behave like an animal.

St Helens man, who is not a saint, is looking for an angel to enjoy romantic evenings in with, watching football and rugby on Sky and listening to *A Book at Bedtime* on the wireless, preferably in bed.

Professor of English Literature seeks an educated lady to watch him play darts on Thursday evening in Eccles.

Lady from Leigh likes to visit the seaside with a man who has a car.

Tracer from Ashton in Makerfield is looking for a draughtsman who is able to draw on unlimited resources for a good time.

Middle aged teacher who likes walking, dancing and visiting pubs in Bury seeks a lady from Rochdale to broaden his outlook on life.

Retired university lecturer who enjoys discussing theories of evolution, ancient Greek philosophy and speaking Esperanto would like to meet a lady from Platt Bridge with similar interests.

Refrigeration engineer from Earlestown seeks someone to chill out with at the weekend whenever United are playing away.

Romantic chick from Prescot would like to meet a man with taste and charm from the other side of the Mersey, anywhere between Birkenhead and America, preferably the latter."

"Tony, do you make these stories up and if you don't, where do you get them from?"

"Well I found all these in the *Star*. But I have to confess that I might have changed a few details over the weekend."

"I saw something funny at the weekend."

It was Dave, determined not to let Tony have all the limelight.

"We were in Debenhams in Manchester buying some clothes last week. A young lad rushed into one of those little booths and closed the curtain, obviously aiming to try something on, I thought. He had only been in there a couple of minutes when he shouts out loudly.

"Billy, there's no toilet paper in here. Can you get us some?"

At this point Mr Musgrove arrived. He was clearly annoyed to have been late and prevent everybody being paid for doing nothing. In his opinion, humour and work were two things that should never be found together.

His lateness was due to a phone call he had just had from Amsterdam. It had put out of date everything that he had planned to say. But before he could say anything, his secretary was tapping on the window, mouthing that he was wanted on the phone again and without saying a thing he left. As soon as he had gone, Dave looked down at his open hands and said: "This place reminds me of my uncle Ken. He was always sat about at work with loads of time on his hands."

"How come?"

"He was a watchmaker. Do you know what one of his favourite sayings was, eh? I'll do that when I've got time."

"I bet he lived at Clock Face."

"Very good Greeno. I'll put that in the minutes before I clock out."

And with that they all left the room and went back to work.

In the middle of the afternoon Colin returned from Fiddler's Ferry and told Alan that he had some bad news.

His wife hadn't been too well recently. Had she been taken seriously ill? His nephew was in the Army in Iraq. Had he been injured or even killed? Colin had been complaining about pains in his chest and had been for some tests. Had he now received a letter informing him that there might be a need for him to have heart surgery? Although he didn't smoke now, as a young man he had regularly smoked 20 a day. Was that linked to the deterioration of his health and the reason why he was not looking too happy with life?

However, as it turned out, it was nothing associated with his own health or the health of any of his relatives. It was to do with something quite close to home, something to be found at the bottom of his garden.

"They've just started work on Mount Geronimo. They are taking it all away. It'll all be gone within a month."

Some time ago, the Bolton Lane Residents Association had started a petition to save this slag heap. In their view it was an area of scenic beauty, the location of a pond full of exotic fish and a place to appreciate a countryside environment in the middle of the town and more. But soon it was to be no more.

What was going to be put in its place? It could be a whole range of things. It might be an estate of new houses, or maybe a multiplex cinema or even an industrial business park.

There was also the issue of a familiar smell that would soon be gone. As long as he could remember, it had always had the smell of sulphur. This was because Lancashire coal was renowned for its high sulphur content. It also explained why smoke could often be seen rising from many slag heaps in the North West. It was something which was caused by the sulphur igniting, particularly like the one at Little Hulton near Bolton though, where his auntie Agnes once lived. That slag heap was always known as Smokey Hill for obvious reasons.

He remembered however how she never called it a slag heap. Round that part of the world, they were always known as a stuff rook.

Nothing much was said about it or any other accumulation of industrial waste during the rest of the day. Everybody was very busy and Mr Musgrove called in twice to discuss some discrepancies with a couple of timesheets. So it was not until lunchtime the following day that any reference was made to what might happen at the bottom of Colin's garden.

"Do you know what the first thing that will happen once the Council has flattened all the land, Colin? You'll suddenly have a load of new neighbours, all parked in their shiny new caravans and letting their dogs and their kids roam all over your back garden."

"I bet somebody has got his eye on your rabbit already."

"I've heard they are going to build an abattoir on it, a right big one for the whole of Merseyside, I hear."

"Funny place to put an abattoir right next to that home for young offenders they have just got planning permission for."

"They won't build that there, not next to a 24 hour petrol station which one of the big oil companies has got plans for."

Colin knew what their game was. He had joined in games like this himself, when a workmate was facing some apparent misfortune. It was a very Lancashire thing too, something that in an odd way seemed to make things not quite as bad as they might first appear.

The following day he came in with the news that his wife had discovered that a new hospital to replace the Victoria Hospital would be built on the land. The latter was to be financed through a PFI scheme, although he didn't quite know what that was and whether it would make any difference.

So Jennifer proceeded to explain what PFI was: "PFI stands for Private Finance Initiative. It's the new way that a government can get hold of the necessary capital to start building schools and hospitals now, and paying for them over the next 30 or 40 years. These deals are very lucrative for the banks as they will have a guaranteed income for all that time though it's not that good for the tax payer."

"Is this some New Labour thing, Jennifer?"

"No, Cliff. PFIs were first introduced by John Major in 1992. At the time the Labour Party were against them. Now that they have become New Labour they are in favour of them."

"So if both the Conservative Party and the Labour Party think that they are a good idea, then they must be a bad thing" suggested Cliff.

"There's a by-election coming up in London in Brent this Thursday, Jennifer. Who do you think is going to win it?"

Before she could answer Alan's question, Tariq said: "It will probably be the Labour Party again. I know the area quite well. I used to live there when I was a student."

"Don't be so sure, Tariq. There is a lot of opposition to what Tony Blair has done with supporting this invasion of Iraq. Labour might just be in for a shock," Jennifer replied.

"I think it might be a close thing" said Alan. "In fact there is a good chance that the spoilt papers might win it. They always seem to do quite well in London."

"Jennifer, you always seem to know what is going on in the world. So tell me, why are they having this by-election?"

"The sitting member died, Cliff."

"What did he die of, gout?"

"I'm not sure. I think that he might have had a heart attack."

"Probably because somebody had found out about how much he was claiming for his expenses."

"That's something else our group is looking into. Loads of MPs are getting away with murder when it comes to claiming for all sorts of things. Our Mary reckons that some of them are even in danger of getting sent down, if it ever comes right out into the open. Not that it ever will though. No doubt it will all get hushed up."

"So if you lived in Brent who would you vote for, Jennifer? I somehow don't think that it would be for Tony Blair. I don't think that he is on your Christmas card list."

"He isn't."

"Jennifer, I agree with most of what your magazine says about the way that the gap between the rich and the rest of the population is growing wider every day, but what can folk do about it. From what I can see, elections are just a smokescreen, giving the illusion that they have some real say in the matter when really they don't. It looks to me like a big con. Labour, Tory, Liberal, all three parties seem to me to be singing from the same hymn sheet."

"You're right Cliff. We have what you might call an economic dictatorship in this country. In other words, rule by and for the interests of corporate business. There exists a very rich and powerful elite that makes all the main decisions about how the economy is run. It's summed up very accurately by the old saying 'whoever has the gold, makes the rules'.

"Parliament is there to work out the details of how that can be best achieved for this elite. But at the same time they have to make sure that the rest of us are kept under control and happy enough with our lot. But no matter what any government wants to do, it can't ignore the basic contradiction that exists in all free market economies, not even though it has the daily backing and support of a powerful and influential right wing press."

"And what might that contradiction be, Jennifer?"

"Let me describe it like this, Cliff. Firms manufacture products like cars, televisions and washing machines with the aim of selling them to the public. That is the way they make money. Some of this money pays the bills, some gets invested in new technology and some is profit for the owners and the shareholders. One thing that they have to pay every week is their employees' wages. The higher the wages are, the lower the profit. But the problem they have is because the lower the wages are, the less money the public has in their pockets to buy the very goods that the firms want to sell to make a profit.

"Another thing that makes things worse is new technology. Robots have been designed to build cars for example but not only does that reduce the need for humans to work on the production line. These robots never go out and spend any money buying the cars they have built, do they?"

"Well I must admit that I have never looked at it like that."

"On top of that look how computers have put so many draughtsmen and draughtswomen like us out of work. Computer Aided Design clearly has both a good side and a bad side for the employing class as I have just explained."

"You are spot on there, Jennifer. As usual."

"What I have just described is also happening in all the other major countries in the world. It means that whole system is now faced with a problem of over production and increased unemployment and also the growth of excessive wealth in the hands of the few."

"Did you learn all this at Salford, Jennifer? I thought you went there to study electrical engineering."

"Before I went to university I learned a lot from my parents, Colin, and also when I saw what happened to my two uncles and a cousin during the miners' strike in 1984. When I was at Salford I got involved in student politics and since then I've learned an enormous amount about world finance from our Mary. She knows so much about how the world runs from working right at the heart of the finance industry over the last five years. And I also learn a lot about the world from all the books and magazines that I read and also from listening to what you lot talk about in here."

At this point all their discussion stopped with the arrival of Mr Musgrove carrying a fax that he had just received. It listed a number of items that should have been included with a delivery that had been dispatched to an iron foundry in Milan over a month ago. Alan let him rant and rave about this omission and then as soon as he managed to get a word in, Alan told him that the items would have been included in the delivery, if Mr Musgrove hadn't made Alan draw up the list of spares before he had even finished doing all the design work.

Jennifer didn't get the chance to say any more as she had now turned her attention to doing some rather complicated meter compensation calculations and by the time she was satisfied with what she had done, it was clocking off time.

The following morning Colin walked into the office, made one long phone call, collected a few prints and drove off to Fiddlers Ferry Power Station again, the third day in a row that he had gone there. Just after lunch he walked back into the office and the first thing he did was to ask if anybody could guess who he had seen just half an hour earlier.

"The Lord Mayor of Widnes?"

"No."

"The Lord Mayor of Widnes's dog?"

"No."

"The Pope?"

"No."

"Lord Lucan?"

"No. It was Ray French, Dave Hadfield, Mike Stephenson, Phil Clarke and a load of Warrington fans."

On his way back to Ashurst, Colin had driven into the centre of Warrington to see how work on the new Halliwell Jones Stadium was progressing. Then he had called in to see his sister who lived on Winwick Road. Just as he was getting back into his car, he saw a crowd of people walking towards him. It was no ordinary crowd of human beings either but a group of rugby league 'celebrities' who had started out on a sponsored walk in Hull a few days earlier. They were raising funds for the Outward Bound Trust, an organisation which provided opportunities for youngsters from poor backgrounds. Having stayed the previous night in St Helens they were now heading for Widnes, which was their final destination.

Colin knew Ray French quite well and couldn't miss the opportunity to walk along with them all into Warrington. When he got back into work he was full of it. And so the rest of the afternoon passed with various other members of the Drawing Office talking about famous people that they had once known or been in company with.

21. "I was born in Barcelona."

The first day of September was a Monday. It was also Alan's birthday. He had now reached the grand old age of 64. In a year's time he would be an old age pensioner. Thelma decided they would celebrate by him taking a day's holiday and the pair of them repeating what they had done to celebrate his last birthday. They started by having their lunch in the Chippery in Market Street in Wigan. Steak pudding, chips, peas, gravy and a barm cake for two and quite a bit of change out of a £10 note as well. Frank, the old man who ran the place, was there as usual, directing operations, keeping all his girls on their toes as he always did and talking to his customers in his broad Wigan accent. He certainly was an OAP. He could even be 75, never mind 65; it was really hard to tell.

The only bad thing about the Chippery was that they didn't do puddings, so they went into Wigan Market Hall, bought a few goodies from one of the cake stalls there and walked over to Trevor Smith's bookshop where they spent the best part of an hour browsing through the local history section and talking to Trevor, something that Alan always enjoyed.

There were four books on the shelf that appealed to him and since it was his birthday, he decided to buy all four. Theoretically, this time next year he would have much more time on his hands to read them. That would be when he could start catching up on all the books he had bought, some of which he had had with him for over 20 years and were still waiting for him to start on.

They called into The Raven on Wallgate like they had done the previous year, hoping to see Rita, but she wasn't there. The woman behind the bar said she hadn't seen her for a few months and thought that she might have moved from her flat in Whelley up to Chorley, where her eldest son lived. They drove home through Orrell, Post and Billinge and arrived back in Ashurst at just turned four o'clock. As they went past the Town Hall, Alan saw the man who held the highest position in the company standing at a bus stop. It was a very smartly dressed Jack Lomax, who drove the overhead crane in the Main Bay. What was he doing there? Why was he not still at work? Maybe it was his birthday too and he had taken a day off. Probably not. Maybe he had won the pools or won the lottery, but again probably not.

As they walked into the house there was a strong smell of baking coming from the kitchen. In the living room, his granddaughter Joanna was sitting there watching television and holding a birthday card in her hand. She jumped up and ran across the room, gave him the card and put her arms out for him to pick her up. They sat down, Alan looked at the card that she had made for him and then she said to him as she so often did: "Granddad. Can we do a jigsaw?"

Half an hour later, when that was finished, all 20 pieces of it, she had another question for him: "Granddad. Can we play Animals?"

Back at work, the following day before he could even check his e-mails or look in his desk diary, he was confronted by a very enthusiastic Jennifer.

"Morning, boss. At last you are famous."

She gave him a copy of the third issue of her magazine and said: "Your article takes up two whole pages."

His account of how Lord Beeching had been prevented from closing Ashurst Railway Station back in the 1960s was there in all its glory, right across the middle pages. He was both pleased and impressed too, although all he had done was to write down exactly what had happened. His article didn't have any direct link with any of the other articles though. In different ways, they all covered the gap that was growing between the top one per cent of the population and the rest of society. But before he could read it, the phone went. It was Dave Morris ringing from the Meter Room at Didcot Power Station with all his usual questions about 'incorrect' wiring connections.

All morning he kept taking the magazine out of the drawer to have another look at what he had written. But each time, something or someone interrupted him and it was lunchtime before he could do just that. By the time he had eaten his sandwiches and read the article a couple of times, Cliff, having finished his dinner, was reading out loud, as he often did, pieces from his newspaper: "The Government's drive to reduce child poverty is helping the marginally poor, but doing little for the one million children in families at the bottom of the income scale, the charity Save the Children warns today. After research into the extent of deprivation among young people, it found nearly 1 in 10 children have suffered severe and persistent poverty lasting five years or more."

"There's plenty material in today's *Guardian* to put in your magazine, Jennifer;" he said as he passed the paper over to her to look at.

"I've known about that report for a while, Cliff. Our Mary has done a lot of research behind the scenes on it. She's very friendly with one of its authors."

Then she took a copy of her magazine out of her bag, opened it at page five, passed it to him and told him to read an article that also covered the same issue of child poverty in Britain.

"Very interesting article that," he said after reading it and then he flicked through the rest of the pages. When he saw what Alan had written, he burst out laughing: "I kept thinking there was something going on between you two, but I never imagined it was anything like this."

By the end of the day she had sold seven copies, whether it was because of the middle pages or despite them, no-one could be sure.

The first thing Alan did when he arrived home that day was to show the magazine to Thelma. She sat down and immediately read it. Suitably impressed by its contents, she asked him to buy two more copies. She was sure she would be able to sell them to two of the people who worked with her in the local Oxfam shop.

On finishing their evening meal, they decided that they would go to Thatto Heath to see Charlie and show him the magazine as well. He didn't answer his phone when they rang, but that meant nothing. If he was upstairs or outside he wouldn't have heard it anyway. When they knocked on the front door there was no answer. It was still a warm evening and he might be doing a bit of gardening, so they went round the back to see if they could find him, but he wasn't there either. His next door neighbour was though, watering his fruit and vegetables.

"Do you know where Charlie is, Bill?"

The man walked over slowly, wiping his hands on a piece of cloth as he did.

"I'm sorry to have to tell you this, Alan. He was taken ill last night, they took him to St Helens Hospital in an ambulance and he died there this morning. His eldest son Paul has just been round about an hour ago and told me."

What a shock that was to both of them, just like it had been when

Sam had died a few weeks earlier. What a shock indeed, not totally unexpected, but still a great shock.

The funeral service was held a few days later in St Austin's Church. Probably twice as many people were there than had been at Sam's funeral, but then Charlie was much better known having lived, except for during war, in Thatto Heath for nearly all his life. After his dad had been buried in Hard Lane Cemetery, his son Paul asked Alan if he would come round to Charlie's house one evening after work.

"My dad has got a load of stuff upstairs. It's no use to me, but knowing what you are like, you might want some of it. Will you come and have a look at it?"

Alan went the next evening. He was glad he did for there were some absolute quality items to be had. They included the programme for the first Challenge Cup Final at Wembley played in 1929 between Wigan and Dewsbury, the first six issues of the *Rugby Leaguer* published in 1949, an autograph book full of signatures – though many undecipherable, papers providing details of Charlie's Army record and a collection of photographs of pre-war Thatto Heath and Nutgrove.

While he was there, Paul said: "I don't know whether to sell the house now Alan, or rent it out. Do you know anybody at work who might be interested? I don't want any hassle over it though."

Alan told Paul that he would first tell his son Robert. Things were getting serious with Megan, who also seemed to be putting on quite a bit of weight as well. Did this possibly mean that the pair of them might soon be looking for a place in which three people could comfortably live? But when he called round to their flat, he was greeted with the news that they had just decided to buy a house on the High Street in Newton-le-Willows.

Charlie's death upset a lot of people who had known him well and notably Joyce. She had met him no more than half a dozen times, but over the years her husband Sam had talked to her a lot about him. And with Charlie's death coming so soon after Sam's, it reminded her again of the man that she had loved and lost.

Joyce was now visiting Thelma once a week for her computer lessons. She had quickly mastered word processing and soon moved onto the use of the internet. In fact, she was quite a dab hand on the keyboard. The 'lesson' such as it was usually lasted an hour. After that they moved on to doing some cooking with recipes that always required the inclusion of a small amount of wine. No one needed much imagination to learn what happened with the rest of what was left in the bottle.

At work the following day he had hardly any time to take his coat off before the phone rang. On the line was Jennifer, informing him that she had been in an accident in Ashton on her way home the previous evening and had broken her ankle. This probably meant that she would be unable to come to work for at least a month. Alan commiserated with her, told they would all miss her and asked her how she would spend the time.

"Well actually Alan, I was thinking that I could work from home if you want me to. If you bring my computer here, there are plenty of drawings that I could do on that job at Eggborough I had just started on. I'd rather do that for part of each day rather than have any of you lot running your grubby hands all over my keyboard."

So it was agreed that he would go up to her house that evening and take Thelma with him. Both had said to him that they would like to meet, and after Thelma had read Jennifer's magazine, she thought she could easily be encouraged to write material for it too.

When they arrived at the house, a woman, who introduced herself as Jennifer's mother Lucy, answered the door. Alan took the computer and monitor up to Jennifer's bedroom and set it up before briefly explaining what he wanted doing on the first three drawings.

They stayed up there for about half an hour, then came downstairs with Jennifer walking very slowly. In the front room Thelma and Lucy were talking about some of the paintings hanging on the walls. After looking at them briefly, Alan asked Jennifer's mother if they called this their Spanish Room.

"Wrong, yet again, Alan" laughed Thelma.

"All these paintings are not Spanish. They are from Catalonia."

Turning back to Lucy, Thelma said: "He often puts his foot in it, jumping in at things. It's an age thing. He's just had another birthday."

"Don't worry. A lot of people have been in this room and made the same mistake."

Then Lucy went on to say that Jennifer had talked a lot about the two of them and then went on to say that she thought that she might have something in common with Thelma.

"Really, are you from South Wales?"

"No, but knowing what I do about you two from Jennifer, I think that you might find my background rather interesting."

They sat there slightly puzzled, but interested. All the time Jennifer had worked in the Drawing Office, she had often referred to her parents and now Alan and Thelma were going to hear something more about them.

"As a child I always assumed that the two people I called mum and dad were my real parents. They were loving and kind and, along with who I thought were my two brothers, I had a happy childhood, even though times were hard what with the war and then the post-war period of shortages and austerity. However, after my 16th birthday, my mum sat me down one afternoon and told me that she had something important to tell me. It was that they had adopted me during the war and that my real mother was her sister who had died when I was a small baby.

"My real mother had been a nurse on the Republican side in the Spanish Civil War and in 1939 she had returned home to England bringing me with her and clearly was very ill. A week after she arrived here she died.

"So that was how the people who were really my uncle and auntie became my parents. Obviously this came as a big shock to me, but they helped me get over it quite quickly and also I had two big 'brothers' to help me as well.

"When I was 19 I decided to go into nursing and began to train at a hospital in Newcastle. A few years later I started going out with a man who I later married. We bought a house in a place called Pity Me in County Durham and settled down there. You'll get the chance to meet him soon. He is working late tonight, but he'll be home soon.

"After we had moved all our possessions into our new home, we were unpacking everything and I found a rag doll that I had had with me as long as I could remember. It had been packed away in an old suitcase that I had always had as long as I could remember. A few days later I found that the cat had taken a great dislike to this doll and almost ripped it to shreds. When I picked it up off the floor, I saw there were some papers and a couple of photographs sewn inside it.

"Now my husband Bill was very political in those days, well he still is, and one of the things that had always interested him was the Spanish Civil War. What was written on these papers was in the Catalan language, but he managed to get it translated. When he discovered what was written, he was absolutely amazed. It provided information about the little girl who the doll belonged to. Her name was Llucia spelled the Catalan way. It gave her date of birth as 1 September 1938 at an address in Barcelona and the name of her mother and father and four other relatives, just in case the child got separated from her mother. It said that she was leaving Spain to make sure that she didn't have to grow up under Fascism and Franco's murderous thugs. It was dated 14 January 1939, about three months before the end of the civil war.

"Later, Bill's friend made contact with some people from a Catalan community that had settled in Paris. We went over there to see them and I showed one old lady the photograph of me as a baby with my real mother and it brought tears to her eyes. She remembered me leaving and told me how my English mother was not only a nurse in the hospital, but had also showed great courage on the battlefields.

"Another old man I met knew my father. He told me that he was originally from Madrid and had died a hero. We came home, with the intention of going to visit Barcelona later that year, but then I discovered that I was pregnant and so we never went."

At this point Bill arrived and was able to add more about what he knew about his wife's background. Thus, it had been a thoroughly enjoyable evening made even better when he thanked Alan for the way he had treated his daughter at work. Meeting Jennifer and her mother also made a big impression on Thelma. Now she wanted to know more about the Spanish Civil War. There were a few books on the subject at home and no doubt there would be an enormous amount available to view and download on the internet. As they drove home Thelma also remembered that Joyce had once told her about her brother who had fought and been killed in Spain just outside Madrid.

She wondered whether to mention this to Joyce who was coming round for her computer lesson the following day. But then that might not be a good idea just at the moment. Joyce was still mourning the death of Sam, although she didn't give the outward appearance of a grieving widow. But then some people can appear on the outside totally different to what is going on inside them.

A few days later, Mr Musgrove walked into the Drawing Office with some news. He had just been informed by Amsterdam that the contract to supply electrical switchgear to the Bottle Handling Plant in Murcia would need to be looked again because the client wanted major changes to be made to the layout of the building.

Alan had half expected something like this would happen. Talking about Catalonia and the Spanish Civil War at Jennifer's and now there was the possibility of a visit to Spain a few days later. A coincidence of sorts and it was one that could be linked with another coincidence as well.

Over the weekend, his sister Joan had rung to tell him that she and her husband Mick were shortly going to spend a fortnight in Murcia. They had been invited to stay at Mick's sister's house on the edge of the town of Calasparra which was less than an hour's drive from the Bottle Handling Plant. Two pairs of coincidences, certainly ones that dear old Charlie would have loved to have been told about if he had still been alive.

22. E-mails from Amsterdam

For as long as anyone could ever remember, one thing that Wilkinson's Drawing Office had always enjoyed was a regular stream of visitors.

There were always people from the Wiring, Assembly and Machine Shops, coming in to get clarifications on drawings. There were regular visits made by electricians and fitters from the Outside Contracts Division to explain what changes they had made out on site that now needed recording. There were wage clerks from the Finance Office querying what had been put on timesheets and expense forms; and sales reps bringing technical information about their company's latest products.

On odd occasions, a former colleague might call in, often with news about another old work mate. And now that the old canteen had been sold off and become the Ashurst Business Centre, people from other departments often came in wanting to use the kettle and the microwave. Three regulars even came to have their lunch almost every day.

As a result, quite often after Alan had been out at a power station or industrial plant somewhere, the first thing that he might be greeted with on his return the following day, would be the words: "You'll never guess who called in here yesterday."

The Drawing Office was not now in the same place it had been in when Alan had started there back in 1962. Nor was it as big as it was then. At its peak, there had been around 100 draughtsmen in a list that included electrical, mechanical, sheet metal and jig & tool plus five tracers. In overall charge of them all had been the chief draughtsman and assistant chief draughtsman, both of whom then had their own office located between the Electrical and Mechanical sections.

Then the Drawing Office was located on the second floor of the General Office. That building no longer existed, having been demolished in 1993 due to subsidence of the land above the coal seams of the old Southport Edge colliery. Now it was located in a single storey building that was adjacent to the Mersey Street gates. Conveniently close to it was Lindsay's Pie Shop along with a sportswear store, and a garage, all on land that had once housed the

Copper Refinery, the Iron and Brass Foundries, the Apprentice Training School and the Transport Department outside which had always been parked an assortment of lorries, vans, company cars and bikes.

The day after Alan visit to Jennifer's house, a couple of old timers had called in. The first was Tony Robledo. Formerly an electrician in the Copper Refinery, he now travelled around Europe installing and commissioning mechanical handling systems. His visit was about business, because he was now in a situation where he needed some electrical drawing work done. What better than to see if his old mate Alan Greenall could provide any assistance?

He spent an hour explaining what he needed to have drawn up, with Alan making notes that would be good enough to convince Mr Musgrove this could be done by a member of his section and to the financial benefit of the company. By the time they had finished talking, it was almost midday.

"Well, I think it's time I took you out for lunch."

"Very good," replied Alan.

Tony looked at his watch and continued: "I've got to be back in my office in Leyland by three o'clock this afternoon, so if we go out now we could just about manage to eat a five course slap up banquet in..."

He put his hand to his mouth, coughed importantly, wiped his face and continued "Martindale's".

As a result of Tony's visit, Alan reckoned there might be two or three weeks' work for one draughtsman, which was not a lot in the grand scheme of things. It would be useful though, since the details about the next contract had still not been sent from Amsterdam, although over the last fortnight Hugo had sent at least three e-mails detailing things that might need to be considered.

The next visitor was Keith Sanderson, a former mechanical draughtsman. Alan had met him in the post office recently. There Keith had asked Alan how far back copies of drawings were kept. He wanted to get hold of one that he had worked on in 1982, but just for personal reasons. Alan offered to look to see if he could find it. He soon did and had rung Keith and told him when he could come and collect it.

It was ironic that drawings of West Thurrock Power Station had been kept, even though the building itself had now been demolished.

156

After giving his old mate the prints and having made him a drink, Alan said: "Are you still watching the Saints, Keith because if you are, I've never seen you in your old spot for ages. Have you started sitting in the stand?"

"No. Since Super League started, I've stopped watching them."

"Bloody hell, Keith. You surprise me. You of all people. Why? What has happened to you? What don't you like about the game now?"

"How long have you got? I don't like summer rugby, I don't like silly nicknames, I don't like squad numbers and I don't like all the music they play. For me going to the match was always a social thing. I always liked to talk to the people I was stood with. Some people I only ever saw was at the match and now you can't hear yourself talk to them. I don't like having to sit down at some grounds either. All seater stadiums are not all seater. You are sitting down, standing up, sitting down, standing up all the time. I can't have that, not with my bad knees."

"I don't agree with Sky deciding when games are played. I don't agree with limited promotion and relegation. I don't agree with throwing money away on teams in London and everywhere else either. How's that for starters?"

"So if you had been in charge of the RFL in 1995, what would you have done when News Corporation offered the game all that money?

"I would have told them to stuff it."

"And how would that have helped? At the time, over half the clubs were close to going bust and rugby union was about to go openly professional. The game could just not go on in the way it had done for the last 90 odd years."

"Why not? It had been fine ever since I can remember it. No Lancashire Cup, that's another thing should never have been stopped. And where's that cup now? Probably on Maurice Lindsay's mantelpiece, I bet. I've never liked games played on a Friday night or on a Sunday afternoon either. Saturday is best. Always was for me."

"Well, you've said a lot of things Keith. Some I might agree with you on, some of the things I think are utter nonsense."

"So, what do you agree with me on?"

"I don't like squad numbers, silly nicknames, loud music, the shirt changing every season and the away shirt being totally different to the home shirt. But then I know why they have done it."

"Why's that?"

"It's a money-making thing, being able to sell two shirts every season instead of one for a start. The same with putting adverts on the shirts, I don't like that either, but then I don't think the clubs can ignore that as a source of income."

"Anything else?

"All seater stadiums. I like to be able to have the choice whether to sit or stand. Like you, I've always preferred to stand. That's not a problem at Knowsley Road is it, but it is nearly everywhere else. You see the way I look at it is this. In 1995 the game needed a completely fresh start. It needed a big cash injection and it needed to be spread further afield. In fact, the game was mainly only played in parts of South Lancashire, West and East Yorkshire and on the Cumberland coast. It also needed to be played in a lot more schools; to have better coverage on TV and in the national papers and it needed to get the professional and amateur games working more closely together."

"So you are happy with everything are you?"

"No. I've just told you what I am not happy with, but I do like a lot about the modern game. If I wasn't happy, I wouldn't go nearly every week. I like the way you can substitute an injured player. I'm glad to see an end to much of the brutality that used to go on, although I do miss some of the brawls I've seen over the years. I also disagree with Sky having the right to alter the time when games are played and often at short notice, but then he who pays the piper does have the right to choose the tune.

"For me, it's not a case of Super League being all good or all bad. It's more a case of some things being positive and some being negative. Me and you are both in our 60s. We look at the game with fond memories of the past. But we only remember the good bits. I reckoned I must have seen some pretty awful games with unlimited possession and contested scrums at places like the old Athletic Ground at Rochdale and at Odsal in Bradford, stood out with no protection from the elements in the wet and the freezing cold."

"You're entitled to your opinion, Alan. Put like that, I suppose you've got a point; but that doesn't change how I feel about it."

"We live in a totally different world to the one that we grew up in, Keith. Rugby league could not afford to ignore how so much in the world has changed. Every other sport has had to change as well, including soccer. It's the same here at work. When we first started, everybody had a job, decisions were made at work, not in some office in America or in our case Amsterdam.

"Then there was much less entertainment on offer for people than there is now. For us it was just going to the flicks on a Friday night, watching the match on a Saturday and on a Sunday you had to go to Sunday school and church once or even twice as well. Right?"

"I suppose so."

"I'm not saying that everything about modern day life is better for the ordinary person. Some things are better and some things are a lot worse and I think it's the latter rather than the former; that is the way things are heading for us plebs in Britain today."

"It's our new girl that Alan is getting all his fancy new ideas from."

It was Colin, who had been listening to them talk while he ate his lunch.

"Where is she then?"

"She's off work at the moment."

"Is she a rugby league fan?"

"Yes, she follows the Wolves or rather should I say that she follows the team that used to be known as the Wire."

"Anyway, what else do you dislike about the modern world, Keith?"

"There's not much I do like about the modern world."

"I thought that you'd say that. You never did like change. I bet when Workington Town applied to join the rugby league you didn't agree with that either. I bet you said: 'Who wants to go right up there over Shap in the middle of winter and when you have no guarantee of getting back home the same night'. And I bet you moaned again a couple of years later when Whitehaven came in."

Keith was probably too young to remember much about the first few seasons after the war when the two Cumbrian teams had joined the Rugby League, but he probably would have objected if he had known then how far away they both were.

"Do you watch much television when you are at home, Keith?"

"A fair amount. I always watch *the Ten o'clock News* and *Newsnight* that's for sure, *Coronation Street* and *Brookside* and the snooker too when it's on. Why?"

"I'm just surprised that you've got a TV in your house. I thought a wireless would have been good enough for you. And what about

159

central heating or do you still have a coal fire?"

"OK. You've made your point. Thanks for the prints."

"One final question: Are you on the internet?"

"My granddaughter is. I'm not. My eyes couldn't stand looking at a screen all day. And how they can produce an A0 drawing on a computer, I'll never know. How does it do it?"

"It's a long story Keith, so you keep taking your medication and you'll easily reach 65."

"I am 65."

"Well done."

And with that Keith took leave of his old mate and shuffled off to find his car, a vehicle full of electronic gadgetry to help him travel all over the country with such ease that he would never have thought possible when he was much younger.

Back at his desk, there was another e-mail from Hugo, this time asking for Alan's home telephone number, something that Alan was quite happy to provide, although he wondered why Hugo had not rung him at work. Maybe his friend had to speak to him about something he didn't want anybody who worked in Amsterdam to know about. Hopefully, all would be revealed quite soon because if no more work was sent their way soon, the issue of redundancy would almost inevitably rear its ugly head.

23. A Swedish affair

"Alan, do you ever remember somebody called Scott Carter?"

"I do, Howard. He spent some time with us in here when he was an apprentice. He was a bit of a character was Scott. Why, have you seen him? What's he done?"

"He's got his name in the papers."

"*The Star* or *The Reporter*?"

"No. Much better than that. He was in last week's *News of the World*."

Scott worked in the Drawing Office in his last three months of his apprenticeship in 1992. He then worked as an electrician in the Works Maintenance Department for the next five years, before handing in his notice. He then went to work in London and nothing had been heard of him since.

A few weeks ago, early one Sunday morning, he had been walking along the Grand Union Canal in Camden where he was now living. In front of him he saw an old woman shuffling towards him. She reminded him of a match box figure out of a Lowry painting.

Suddenly, a man with a balaclava over his face and wearing a striped jumper and heavy boots had appeared. He looked a right thug. He pushed the woman to the ground, snatched her handbag and began running towards Scott. As he came nearer, Scott had stepped to one side as if to let him pass and then had stuck his leg out. The man went down and the handbag fell to the ground. The thief had struggled to get up and appeared torn between running away and getting hold of the handbag. But Scott had been too quick for him to do either. He grabbed hold of him and begun to push him towards the water. As he did, he heard a loud shout coming from behind him.

He turned round and saw two policemen running towards him. By their appearance they looked more like old fashioned policemen from the 1930s. Well, that was what they were, so to speak.

It turned out there was a camera crew on a bridge over the canal behind Scott, filming a scene for a film that was being made by a Swedish television company. Whoever was in charge decided that the incident involving Scott and the 'thug' was better than what had been intended as the original story line. She also took an immediate liking to Scott and invited him to have breakfast with her in the crew's mobile canteen parked nearby. Then he had another stroke of luck. While they were talking, a fuse had blown on one of the lighting circuits and the Swedish electrician was nowhere to be found. Scott told her that he could fix it, which he did, and before the day was out he was on the pay roll in his combined role as a film extra and site electrician.

On location for the next two weeks, Scott began to sweet talk Ingrid and, despite her being some 20 years older than he was; they soon began to have more breakfasts together, sometimes in her flat in West Hampstead. With his assistance, she began to rewrite parts of the film which began in Stockholm, moved to London, and finished up in a northern cotton town before returning to Sweden, all during the run up to the outbreak of the Second World War in 1939.

Ingrid was well known in Swedish high society and this helped contribute to the rise of Scott, who had begun to milk it for all he was worth. One thing that helped him was his Nook End accent. People from that part of Ashurst had a very distinctive way of speaking, which seemed to have gone down well with all the people in whose company he was now operating. Neither Ingrid nor any of the others had a clue about all the different English accents that existed in the 1930s and so as far as they were concerned, Scott was an expert.

"I'm not surprised that something like that's happened to him. He was always acting all the time he worked here. Sometimes, he used to act as though he was a draughtsman, but most of the time he used to act the goat or like a nine year old child."

"Was he a bit of a man for the ladies as well?"

"He certainly was. Make a big impression with someone with the very first words that you say to them. Then get them talking about themselves. I remember him telling me some of the opening chat up lines he used. Let's see what I can remember."

'Hi, I am Mr Wright. I believe that you have been looking for me.'

'Do you believe in love at first sight or should I walk past you again?'

'Do you like raisins? No? Well, how about a date then?'

'You remind me of a magnet because you have just attracted me over here.'

'Well here I am. What were your other two wishes?'

"I'm not sure though how much a Swedish woman old enough to be his mother would appreciate or even understand them, but clearly she must be appreciating something that he's got."

Alan told Thelma about Scott while they were eating their evening meal later. She had never met Scott, although she knew about him because Alan had often told her about his various scrapes. She then told him that Phil had been round earlier and wanted him to help move some furniture which he and Janice had brought back from Oldham that afternoon.

As soon as that had been done, bottles of German beer appeared and their first item of conversation was about what Keith had said to Alan at work about him no longer watching the Saints.

"I might agree with him on some things Alan, but then I don't think that the game had much of an alternative. It would probably have gone bust if we hadn't accepted what News Corporation offered. In my opinion, where it all went wrong was handing all the money over to the clubs that were going into Super League. The money should have been put into a separate bank account while there had been a proper debate about how it should be used. Instead, a lot of players made a fortune out of it.

"In my opinion, if we had rejected the News Corporation money, Murdoch might easily have decided to bang it all into rugby union. Another possibility was that he might have used it to encourage some union clubs and some league clubs to merge and produce a hybrid game. When a man has got so much money and so much power that goes with it as he had, he can do what he wants and that is what he could have done if he had wanted to."

"I told Keith that I thought it was a case of some things being better and some things being worse. I think that the move to playing in the summer was a good idea, but on the other hand, the way the game tried to win over many younger people alienated a lot of older fans. Once upon a time I used to love talking to people who I only ever used to see at the match. You can't really do that now. The noise is far too loud."

"You're right, Alan. Last week, I met an old mate from Nook End who told me he never goes now and said something to me that I thought was really sad: 'No matter what these buggers do, they'll never take my memories away.'"

"Well he's right to a degree. Everything we all did as kids seems better then than what's on offer now, but it probably wasn't."

"I think you're right. Why would you want to remember all the bad things?"

"So when did you start watching the Saints, Phil?"

"It was 1953, the year they went to Wembley. We lived in McFarlane Avenue and my dad used to go every week and sometimes took my brother with him. My uncle and my cousin used to go as well. They lived on Ellison Drive so they could all just walk there together. When I had just turned seven my dad said that I could start going with them. I can still remember that day so well. We stopped outside the boy's pen; my dad gave our kid a shilling and said that he would wait for us both when the game was over. Then he said a strange thing to me. He asked me to see if I recognised number three. Well I didn't have a clue what a number three was.

"We got right to the front and soon after the two teams ran on to the field. That was when I saw that the players all had numbers on the back of their jerseys. After about 10 minutes the other team must have scored a try and all the Saints players came and stood behind the posts right near to where we were. I had a good look at number three and I recognised him straightaway.

"Our kid told my mother later what I did. I shouted out 'Mr Greenall, Mr Greenall. I'm watching the Saints.'"

"It was Duggie Greenall. My dad worked with him at Triplex and he had been to our house a few times before. Memories, eh."

Their conversation then moved on to how Phil was spending his time, now that he no longer had to go to Hilton's every day.

"Thanks to Janice, I've started doing some painting, which I find very relaxing. I've started doing a lot more cooking and I'm learning to speak Italian, which she speaks quite fluently and I've even been to an art gallery in Liverpool. In fact Alan, I don't know how I ever found the time to go to work."

"That old favourite."

"Well it's right, well it is for me, but I don't think everybody enjoys retirement. But I think you will. In fact I'm sure of it."

The following evening, Alan received a phone call from Hugo, telling him what had just been decided by the board. The company was now in severe financial difficulties. As a result the main storage warehouse had been sold to a property developer from Rotterdam and next week the board would be discussing what they were going to sell off next. They had interests and links with companies in Belgium and France as well as England and everything was at risk.

"You don't need to know how I have found all this out, Alan. And don't let anybody know that I told you all this either. Keep it to yourself, but I just thought that you ought to be aware of what might happen in the very near future, probably by the end of this month. You are my friend and friends should help each other."

And with that the line went dead and Alan never heard from his Dutch friend again.

24. "Is there any future after this?"

"Listen up everybody. Jennifer is coming in today for a bit, so can you all make the place look a lot more untidy so that she'll feel at home when she gets here."

Jennifer had been off work for nearly a month now. In her absence the general atmosphere in the office had gone down, but it soon went up again when she hobbled in on crutches a couple of hours later. By the time she had finished talking to Alan about what he wanted her to work on next, it was lunchtime and hopefully time for some interesting conversation. It always was when she was around and it started with Cliff asking her what she had been doing while she had been off work.

"Reading, writing and watching weeds in the garden grow."

"So what have you written then, a GET ILL card for our beloved section leader maybe?"

"No. I've written an article for the next issue of our magazine."

"Go on then, tell us about it, then we won't have to buy a copy when it comes out."

"It's called "Unemployment doesn't work". It's a review of how bad the policies of the Thatcher Government were for most of the people who lived in the north of England in the 1980s."

"What was wrong with Mrs Thatcher? The economy was in a right mess when she was elected thanks to the previous Labour Government. Like running a shop, you can't spend more than you've got coming in. That was what Labour were doing, same as every other Labour Government has always done, wasting other people's money."

These words were said by Ken Smith. He worked in the Technical Publicity Department and was there looking for information from a technical manual that was always kept in the Drawing Office. He was a nice enough sort of a bloke, but one always prepared to believe and defend whatever he read in his copy of the *Daily Mail*.

"Ken, that sounds pretty much like a press release from the Conservative Party HQ."

Ignoring what Alan had just said, he went on: "We were paying ourselves more than we could afford. We were wasting money being in the Common Market, the coal and the steel industries were losing money hand over fist and the unions thought the world owed them a living. Mrs Thatcher knew all this and was prepared to do something about it. What was wrong with what she did?"

"And I suppose that you would have still agreed with her, even if you had lost your job and had never been able to find a job again."

"Cliff, there's always work for those who want it. All those people who said they couldn't find work didn't want to work. They were all better off on the dole. And I see that you haven't said anything about Tony Blair. He's just as bad."

"You mean he's just as bad as Margaret Thatcher. So you do believe that she was bad? Looks like Jennifer has convinced you already."

"Look Alan, I don't want to get involved in any political discussion here. I don't believe that politics should be discussed at work. Work is where you are supposed to do some work. Politics is a private matter, one between a man and his ballot paper."

"Don't women have any say in the matter, then in your view?"

It was Jennifer keen to expand on what she had just said: "Politics is not a private matter, Ken. It's a very public matter and it's not just about putting a cross against the name of some well-heeled politician who rarely manages to do what he promises to do, when he is elected. Politics is all about how a society should be run in the interests of the people and how it looks after the most vulnerable.

"Just look at what Thatcher did and see how it affected the north west. During her time as Prime Minister, unemployment went up from around 1.2 million to over three million, British manufacturing capacity was halved and council houses were sold off by local authorities who were not allowed to use the money they received to build any new houses. She broke up the power generation and transmission industry. She did the same with the Gas Board. Thanks to her, we saw the biggest ever transfer of wealth from the population at large to the rich in British history."

"She's right, Ken. Your own sister got affected by politics when she got finished at Mather's, didn't she? Your lad got affected by politics too. He couldn't get a job because there were none and had to join the Army and now he's involved in this illegal war in Iraq. Once upon a time you could catch a bus from your house into town every 20 minutes. Then that route was given to a private company to run and because they can't make enough money out of it, they stopped running buses up to Helmsley after six o'clock."

"I know what I think and no lefty talk about what Mrs Thatcher did 20 years ago is going to get me to change my mind about her. And by the way it was that stupid union man from Bolton that closed Mather's down, whatever his name was."

"I thought it was that dodgy director from the Isle of Man who caused it with one of his dubious financial deals."

Soon after, Ken went back to his own office, though he probably went outside first to have a smoke, something he did about a dozen times every day. With him gone Jennifer went on to add a bit more to what she had just said: "In the 70s, Keynesian economic ideas were being overthrown by supporters of the Chicago School Free Market Model with their views about how to help corporate business make super profits, despite the social cost that came with it. Remember Nigel Lawson saying that unemployment was a price worth paying. The unions had to have whatever power they still had, reduced and state monopolies had to be broken up and turned into separate private money making ventures, with large parts of them now foreign owned. Stopping free school milk for primary schoolchildren was another thing that she did and she was able to get away with it because she had the enthusiastic support every day from a strong and very biased right wing press.

"She was also lucky because around the time she was elected, North Sea oil was beginning to come ashore in large quantities. The high price of oil which had almost crippled Callaghan's Government provided high revenues for her to use. It brought about an end to the balance of payments deficit that had dogged the British economy for decades. She could have invested some of that wealth in our manufacturing industries. But instead, she promoted the finance industry. It was a disastrous decision and we can see the result of that now all across the north of England with the total decline of engineering."

"How do you get all this information, Jennifer?"

"I read a lot of books and magazines Tariq. I watch good quality programmes on the TV. I listen to my parents talk about what things were like for them in the past and I can see what is happening all around me. I also learn a lot from our Mary and both of us want to do something about it and not just be passive observers."

"Well, you are certainly not that. It's a pity there are not a lot more people like you around."

"It was interesting to hear what Ken said about Tony Blair as well. In moving the political landscape to the right, Mrs Thatcher ironically contributed to bringing about New Labour. Tony Blair is just as committed as she was to the free market economy. In fact I was thinking of calling my article. 'New Labour. My greatest achievement' or maybe even 'Blair, child of Thatcher!' Maybe I still will."

Before she could say much more, Dawn rang from reception to tell her that her neighbour had just arrived and was ready to drive her back home to Wigan.

She wished them all the best for the weekend and asked Alan to try and be a gentleman for once and carry her bag that contained a bunch of papers that she needed for her next set of drawings.

As he ate his lunch Alan recalled what he had first thought about Jennifer when he had interviewed her for the job that she was now doing so well. She had all the necessary qualifications, much better than the other people who he had seen. However, at first he wasn't sure how well she would fit into an office full of men; but within a week he was well pleased that he had chosen her. She had helped improve the general atmosphere in the office and soon everybody was learning a lot from her views about the world in which they all lived.

In fact, she only appeared to have one fault. It was her untidiness, she was almost as bad as Howard and that took some doing.

Then he thought about the future and what he might be doing in a little more than a year's time. Would the rest of them still be here? Who would be in charge, might they even ask him to stay on? Would he stay on if they asked him to? On the other hand would the place still be here? He didn't know. How could he?

Over the previous weekend he had met another old work mate who told him that he was having the time of his life, playing golf, bowling, taking the grandchildren out, all five of them, but only one at a time. Terry was also building a shed at the bottom of his garden and had orders to build something similar for two of his daughters. He was also trying to some find time to visit his son who lived on a farm in Cornwall. And Alan remembered the last few words Terry had said to him as they were stood in the queue in ASDA, the same words that

Phil had used: "I don't know how I ever found the time to go to work."

Alan then thought of some of the places he fancied visiting once he was retired, Sydney on the east coast of Australia was one. Thelma could meet her cousin Laurie and maybe other people who had once known her father. They could also watch a few Australian rugby league games, certainly ones that featured a distant relative who now played for Manly.

He also fancied spending time in the south of France, Albi, Carcassonne and Perpignan, all beautiful towns each with a good local team to watch. And if his sister Joan and her husband Mick did decide to go to live in Spain, there would certainly be an invitation for them both to stay there as well.

As soon as he had finished his lunch he walked into town to do some shopping and when he returned he found Cliff sat at his desk.

"Musgrove has just rung. It turns out that Amsterdam were too quick making all the people in that drawing office in Antwerp redundant. A problem has cropped up on a job in Venezuela they were all working on and one of us has to go and sort it out. He also wants us to organise the removal of everything from that mill in Accrington.

"I told him if you had to choose, you would almost certainly want to deal with that so I've got to go and spend a month in Caracas. So you won't mind if I leave early this afternoon and go and buy some sun tan lotion and try and find my passport, will you?"

Mr Musgrove reappeared around half past three and by the time he had left, everybody else had gone home. Alan switched off all the lights, walked out of the building and decided to buy a copy of the *Evening Post* at the newsagents on the other side of the road. He waved to the gateman Frank who mouthed something to him through his window. Whatever it was Alan didn't know, but it didn't matter. He could ask Frank what he had said when he came back to his car with his paper in a few minute's time.

Stood on the pavement he saw a brightly coloured lorry approaching and as it passed him, he noticed the Amsterdam address on its side. Another Charlie Eccleston coincidence, he thought. As he prepared to step off the pavement, behind the lorry he saw a van approaching with its nearside indicator flashing, showing that the driver was going to turn into the factory. He glanced left again then walked slowly onto the road, unaware that the van driver did not know that his indicator was on when he wasn't going to turn left into the factory.

Frank was on the phone seconds later, ringing 999 for an ambulance to come as fast as it could. There had been what looked like a terrible accident right outside Lindsay's pie shop on Mersey Street. And Frank knew well the man who would surely urgently need their immediate attention.

Other books from London League Publications Ltd:

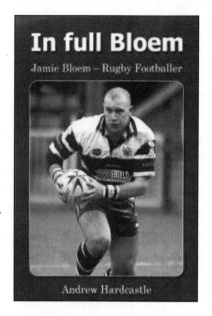 

In full Bloem: The explosive biography of Jamie Bloem, current referee and former Halifax player. Published in February 2013 @ £14.95 (hardback), just £14.00 post free in the UK direct from London League Publications Ltd.

Heading for the line: Great new guidebook for rugby league grounds, published in April 2013 @ £7.95 (paperback), just £7.50 post free in the UK direct from London League Publications Ltd.

Geoff Lee's novels *One Winter* and *One Autumn* are available from London League Publications Ltd post free in the UK @ £9.00 each (paperbacks); published @ £9.95.

All our books can be ordered from any bookshop @ full price. To order direct from London League Publications Ltd visit our website: www.llpshop.co.uk or write to LLP, PO Box 65784, London NW2 9NS (cheques payable to London League Publications Ltd).